April
To: Rachel ;

FACES BEHIND THE DUST

Enjoy

Ora L. Hairston

Faces Behind the Dust

The Story Told Through The Eyes Of A Coal Miner's Daughter
(On the black side)

Cora L. Hairston

iUniverse, Inc.
Bloomington

FACES BEHIND THE DUST
The story told through the eyes of a coal miner's daughter
(on the black side)

Copyright © 2013 by Cora L. Hairston.

All rights reserved. No part of this book may be used or reproduced by any means, graphic, electronic, or mechanical, including photocopying, recording, taping or by any information storage retrieval system without the written permission of the publisher except in the case of brief quotations embodied in critical articles and reviews.

This is a work of fiction. All of the characters, names, incidents, organizations, and dialogue in this novel are either the products of the author's imagination or are used fictitiously.

iUniverse books may be ordered through booksellers or by contacting:

iUniverse
1663 Liberty Drive
Bloomington, IN 47403
www.iuniverse.com
1-800-Authors (1-800-288-4677)

Because of the dynamic nature of the Internet, any web addresses or links contained in this book may have changed since publication and may no longer be valid. The views expressed in this work are solely those of the author and do not necessarily reflect the views of the publisher, and the publisher hereby disclaims any responsibility for them.

Any people depicted in stock imagery provided by Thinkstock are models, and such images are being used for illustrative purposes only.
Certain stock imagery © Thinkstock.

ISBN: 978-1-4759-5829-4 (sc)
ISBN: 978-1-4759-5830-0 (ebk)

Library of Congress Control Number: 2012920143

Printed in the United States of America

iUniverse rev. date: 11/20/2012

Pauline Stokes comments, I truly believe this book is a hit. I have laughed from talking to my "aunt" as she read some of the pages to me over the phone. I can picture my old home place while she reads to me. I am looking forward to the full book to laugh until my sides hurt."

Antoinette Montgomery says, I am excitedly anticipating the finished product of my friend's book. She has given me some insight and I have laughed until I cried. So I know I'm going to have to have a box of Kleenex next to me as I read the book in its entirety. Congratulations "girlfriend." NOW, GIT UR DONE WHY DON'T YA!!

Kenneth Nunley says, I had the privilege of having read the book in its entirety. Cora and I have been friends for years. We happened to meet up one Saturday while out shopping and in talking she mentioned that she was writing a book. Well, as it so happens I've written several and I recommended this company to her. She entrusted me to read over her product after completion and comment on any changes I thought she should make. I did, and I told her to change nothing because it's the life in the "coal fields" as told through the eyes of this little nosey girl. I think she has a hit on her hands.

Contents

Chapter 1	My Daddy's Love	1
Chapter 2	Mama (My Thea-Thea)	4
Chapter 3	Play Time (the Real Miss *Meee*)	8
Chapter 4	Minding My Own Business	12
Chapter 5	The Marriage (uggggh)	18
Chapter 6	Mr. Man's Family	24
Chapter 7	What the World? What the World!	29
Chapter 8	The Crow Pole	32
Chapter 9	HoneyBabe	37
Chapter 10	Coal Miner's Talk	40
Chapter 11	My Little Boo	42
Chapter 12	Communities	44
Chapter 13	Love Has No Color	47
Chapter 14	How Olive Came to Be	49
Chapter 15	No Love Like Mother Love	52
Chapter 16	Time with My Ludie	54
Chapter 17	Good Old Ms. Maxwell	56
Chapter 18	Weirdo!	60
Chapter 19	Combing through the Forest	63
Chapter 20	The Wooden Throne	65
Chapter 21	Living for the Weekend	67
Chapter 22	Yippee!	71
Chapter 23	Summertime, Summertime	76

Chapter 24	Oh Brother, You Know Better	88
Chapter 25	Bee-Bee and Boo	91
Chapter 26	What the World, What *the World!*	94
Chapter 27	The Funeral	100
Chapter 28	The Uncle I Never Knew	105
Chapter 29	Change Gonna Come	108
Chapter 30	Hear No Evil, See No Evil	111
Chapter 31	A Whole New World	114
Chapter 32	Halfway (completely different)	116
Chapter 33	Looking for Love	119
Chapter 34	Time Marches On	122
Chapter 35	Tragedy	125
Chapter 36	Spoiled?	130
Chapter 37	Praise the Lord . . . I Think	135
Chapter 38	Oh Brother	142
Chapter 39	Whoopee!	145
Chapter 40	Hog-Killing Time & Holidays	152
Chapter 41	Christmas!	157
Chapter 42	Back to the Nitty Gritty	166
Chapter 43	Not My Ludie, Lord!	168
Chapter 44	Growing Up, *Uh-Oh*	174
Chapter 45	Change Is Coming	177
Chapter 46	The Big Move	180
Chapter 47	Graduation	191
Chapter 48	Had Enough	195
Chapter 49	Yippee!	199

I would like to dedicate this book to my husband Fred, who sat and laughed at me and with me when I would read from the pages as I wrote. He would shake his head and say, "girl, where do you come up with such stuff." His advice and presence were very helpful as he is a retired "coal miner."

Also, I dedicate this book to "Isaac Newton Perkins," whom we lost at the tender age of 26 to the same vicious brain tumor that took the life of Senator Ted Kennedy. I know he is in Heaven shaking his head saying uhm, uhm, uhm, grandma, grandma, grandma. (smile.)

I truly want to thank Shelia McGhee, my "Eastern Star Sister." On June 29, 2012, we attended the 98th Grand Communication session held in Martinsburg, WV. While there, I asked my sisters to give me suggestions for the title of my book.

After morning session she hurriedly came up to the organ with glee on her face saying excitedly, "I've got it!!" "Faces Behind The Dust!!" "Oh, she says, I've got goose bumps!" Well, so did I. Thank Shelia.

I want to thank Kenneth Nunley my friend whom I've known for years for his advice, and also for proofreading my book. Love you.

Thanks to all well wishers and others too.

This is an open-ended book with more to come. So grab a cold one, a hot cup of java, or a hooch, sit down, prop your feet up, and get ready to laugh, cry, or whatever else this book makes you feel like doing . . . but most of all, enjoy.

Chapter One

MY DADDY'S LOVE

Sitting at the kitchen table with my chin in my hands, watching my mama, Thea-Thea, work her magic, knowing I was getting ready to get my grub on, I looked up at the clock and panicked.

"*Run,* Junior, *run!*" I screamed. "The *Man-Trip* is coming out of the hole!"

Junior flew around the house from where he was helping our older brother, Russell churn ice cream on the back porch and joined me as I was already running down the hill.

My daddy was coming home! *Calvin Mickens, yep, that's my daddy.* I ran as fast as my little legs would go.

It was the heart of summer, and I was huffing to greet my daddy, who was coming home from another hard day down in the dark pits of the coal mine. He always saved something from his lunch for us, and no matter how small it was, it was shared between the two of us—my brother Junior and me. Russell was fifteen years old and felt he was too old to act like a kid, so it was just that much more for me and Junior. Junior is ten years old, almost eleven and I am five years old going on six and smart too. We've both got birthdays coming up. Our big sis, Evelyn—she was too old to care about silly things like that too—she was in *looovve* and getting married soon.

There were six children total—four boys and two girls—and I was the B-A-B-Y of the brood. There were only four of us at home now. My two oldest brothers, Oscar and Frank, were married. At least I think they were—they had two old bags they lived with, and

I couldn't stand neither one of 'em! But never mind; I'll get back to them later . . . .

Daddy was walking down the hill with the rest of the men, grinning from ear to ear. I could only see the whites of his eyes and his big white teeth, as he—just like all the others—was completely black, covered with coal dust. You couldn't tell the white men from the black men until you got close to them, or heard them talk. But me, *huh*, I would know my daddy *anywhere*!

The men were from different parts of the world. Daddy said some of the white men were from Poland, Germany, Yugoslavia, and other strange places, and he could hardly understand them, because they spoke very little English. His other white buddies just had that hillbilly slang that stood out from the Southern drawl of my daddy and the other black men. Everybody was unique in their own way.

We were the apples of my daddy's eye, and we knew it.

"*Run ClaraBy, run!*" Ludie screamed as loud as she could, urging me to catch up. Ludie was my very best friend in the whole wide world. She is sickly. She was born with some rare disease and had been sick all of her young life, only having gone to school for two years. But she was smart as a whip. She would read to me all of the time.

I didn't know what was wrong with her, and I didn't understand what they meant when I was told that she might not live to be an adult. When the grownups were talking about her, everyone would hush and change the subject if I came around. So I just ignored it, I guess.

"*Last one there is a snail!*," Junior yelled as he ran ahead of me, grabbing Daddy's lunch bucket.

Daddy's lunch bucket was special. I made sure it was clean every day after we ate the morsels Daddy had left. Thea-Thea made sure that she packed extra just for us to have. Daddy's bucket consisted of three parts: a tin top on top of a tin tray for the food that sat on top of the tin bucket for his drinking water. The lid fit tightly over the tray and the bottom, so as not to spill the water.

Daddy said, "Hello, son." patting Junior on the head. When I finally reached him panting, I wrapped my arms around his leg and clung on while he said the words that were magic to my ears, "Hello, princess."

"Hi Daddy!" I said, as he dragged me all the way home to the steps. Then and only then would I let go of his leg, my daddy's leg, my hero's leg.

He was small in stature, but he was a giant to us, and everybody knew he did not take *no junk.* Calvin Mickens made it plain and clear that there were three things that belonged to him and you didn't mess with: his wife, his children, and his money in that order. He worked hard for his family.

Thea-Thea, was standing on the porch, wiping her hands on her apron, waiting for Daddy to come up the steps as she did every day, winter and summer.

He always looked at her with love in his eyes as he gently kissed her on the cheek and said, "Hi, HoneyBabe," his pet name for her. She always replied, "Hello, handsome," as she took his hard hat." They went into the house, and me and Junior; we stayed on the top steps and ate our snack.

Russell, who thought he was something, being over six feet by now, greeted him at the door and gave Daddy a big handshake and a pat on the head, saying, "Hey Pops."

Daddy beamed as he looked up at him and said, "Hello son."

My big sister, Evelyn, whom we called just that, "Big Sis," was in the kitchen getting supper ready. "Hey Daddy!" she said, grinning from ear to ear and giving him a peck on the cheek. "We got supper almost ready, and some homemade ice cream to boot!" she said excitedly as she ran upstairs to lay out her evening date wear.

Daddy went to bathe, saying, "Now dat sounds good, Big Sis. "I sho can use dat cold, ice cream today . . . . Whee, it's a scorcher out there!"

And Thea-Thea replied, "Sho-nuff is."

Chapter Two

MAMA
(My Thea-Thea)

Thea-Thea is an odd nickname, and everybody called her that. I was told that it is an old name passed down through the ages in our family from our Indian ancestors—don't ask me what it means, nobody ever said, it just was. She was the most precious thing in all of our lives, my mama, Delores Ann Mickens.

She was a beautiful thing, with black, kinky, curly locks of hair that hung past her shoulders, thick as lambs wool and just as soft, which she had pinned up in a pile on top of her head because, she said, it was hot. When she washed it and greased it down, it hung in ringlets of curls until it dried.

She was the color of a cup of black coffee with cream—but not too much cream, if you know what I mean. She was the most beautiful shade of brown I have ever seen. The Indian and African-Negro blood had made a beautiful specimen. She had high cheek bones and lips that needed no lipstick—they looked as if she kept lipstick on—and hazel eyes that seemed to look into your very soul. And very feisty—she was a woman of her word. If she said it, you could rely on it.

She was proud of her Indian blood and often spoke of her ancestors in Virginia. She would often say, "One of these days, I'm gonna look up my Injun cousins and such, ya know. I'd really like to do dat someday." She was soft-spoken, petite and medium-built with a tiny waistline and big hips. I would often catch Daddy hitting her on the behind and her giggling like a school girl. The hips are a trademark in our family as the Negro girls were well endowed.

At night, as we sat around, no matter what we were doing, I would be sitting close to her, sucking on my bottom lip, kneading the upper part of her arm, which was soft and flabby, until I fell asleep. Thea-Thea said it was my sleeping aide.

She hums a happy tune as she finishes supper. Daddy sat in his work chair behind the coal stove in the kitchen, winter and summer, and removed his steel-toed boots and *bankers*—shirt, pants, underwear socks—his wide leather belt, hardhat, gloves, and the rest of his work gear, and laid them in a pile on the floor to be worn again the next day. They were heavily laden with black coal dust.

The *bankers,* as the miners called their clothes, were washed maybe once or twice a month. Calvin Mickens had two changes of them, so when one was in the laundry, he wore the other. I can only imagine how some of the miners' bankers were never washed . . . especially J. J. and Sarah's daddy, Mr. Monroe. Their daddy didn't take very good care of his family. I had overheard the grownups talk about how he wasted the money he made and never drew a payday. Their mother did the best she could with what she had to work with. J.J. and Sarah hardly had anything it seemed. So everyone in the community looked out for them.

We were one of the fortunate families. We had a wringer washing machine and two washboards. Thea-Thea would rub the clothes that needed extra attention on the boards, dip them down in the tub of water, bring them back up, and rub some more. Her hands would sometimes be red as fire. Then she would put them in the clean water in the wringer washer. The clothes came out sparkling clean and smelled so fresh when brought in off the clothes lines. She always hummed one of the old Negro Spirituals when she worked. She had a beautiful soprano voice, which seemed to keep her perked up. She never seemed to get tired . . .

My daddy was a proud coal miner and a staunch union man. He wore his bankers with pride, like a soldier in his uniform. He always came upstairs and looked down on us when we were asleep, and just turned and walked back downstairs before he went to work. If I was awake, I'd rub my sleepy eyes as he bent down to kiss my cheek. If he had on his clean bankers, I'd reach up and give him a big hug. *That's my daddy!*

Thea-Thea and Big Sis had prepared the table for supper before Daddy took his bath behind the stove. Putting on fresh white long johns, which he wore all year round—how, I don't know, as there was no such thing as an air conditioner, but he never seemed to get hot—he came from behind the stove and said, "Ahhh boy, dat feels good," and headed for the table.

The old fan that sat on top of the cabinet was definitely off limits for anybody to touch but Thea-Thea or Daddy, as it was dangerous, having no cover to protect you from getting your fingers cut—or worse—cut off.

Thea-Thea called us to supper, "ClaraBy, Russell, Junior, come and eat!"

Mmm mm, my Thea-Thea could cook. It was summertime and any vegetable on the table was grown in our huge garden behind the outhouse. Okra, greens of every description, green beans, onions, beets, corn as tall as a tree, potatoes, tomatoes, onions—you name it, we grew it, even watermelons.. If we didn't grow it, the boys would go find it in the wild. They were good at it too! They brought back whatever was in season.

Today, we were having poke salad, hot biscuits, pork chops, gravy, and mashed potatoes. For desert, we had homemade ice cream. Hot coffee for Daddy and Thea-Thea, sweet water for us. Yum, Yum, Yum

Russell and Junior always enjoyed churning the old ice cream maker, taking turns and fussing over who cranked the longest. I just wanted them to get it done.

Thea-Thea had gotten an extra block of ice from the ice-man who had run early that morning and put it in the ice box that sat on the back porch. She had chipped me off some and put it in a bowl. I danced and sang as I chomped on the ice until it was all gone. Then I got bored waiting. *"Git wit it!"* I hollered.

"You *git* in the house!" Russell shot back.

I went in the house huffing and puffing, and plopped down at the table twiddling my thumbs, twisting my hair around my fingers, crossing and uncrossing my legs. But then my mind forgot about my stomach as I ran for my little life to greet my daddy.

Thea-Thea had a way of making anything taste good. While I sat at the table watching her work her magic with the food, I became curious. "Thea-Thea, what you doing that for?"

She said, "Well, I'm squeezing da water outa da poke-salad since it's done been par-boiled, and I'm gonna fry it in bacon grease wit fresh green onions."

"Oooh," I said, curiosity cured.

We were always treated with at least one *mess* of poke salad a season. This green leafy vegetable grew wild all over the place.

Russell and Junior had gone poke-salad picking and had made a good little piece of change selling it around the neighborhood. It was good medicine the old folks said.

"Yeah right," I'd say, because it made me have the runs, which Thea-Thea said was good for us to have a good cleaning out. Well, I know my little butt was sore from the trips to the outhouse.

The biscuits, were delicious hot or cold. She always made a pan of biscuits with a *hoe cake* at the top. The hoe cake—a biscuit that is much bigger and longer at the head of the long bread pan, sort of a loaf biscuit—was for Daddy and Daddy only; we all knew that.

Daddy would always wait until us kids had gotten our food on our plates before he would fix his plate. We children never knew why until later years, when Thea-Thea told us that it was because he'd had so little as a child that he wanted to make sure we had as much as we wanted. They just don't make 'em like my daddy anymore, no sirreeee.

Chapter Three

PLAY TIME
(the Real Miss *Meee*)

Supper finished, table cleared by the boys and me, Big Sis is left to wash the dishes. Time to go play, but only after we finish our chores. Russell and Junior had to chop wood, fill up the coal buckets and carry them in the house, clean out the cook stove, which by now had cooled down some so they could shovel out the ashes carry them out, and prepare it for the next day. I helped carry wood like the big girl I thought I was, and bring in the slop jar for the night. Then I would visit with my pet piglet Little Red. She was the cutest thing I had ever seen. I fed her every morning and evening. She looked for me.

I had the dirtiest job in the whole house, I thought, emptying the 'slop jar.'

Russell said, "Baby Girl, you ain't the only one that had that job. I had to do it before Junior had it, and now it's your turn. When it gets too heavy, we'll help you carry it out."

"Okay," I mumbled, and then I thought to myself, "What a crock; I am only five, almost six years old . . . *geeeeee* already." My favorite job, though, was helping with the wood. I was proud to be helping.

"Don't carry too much at one time, Baby Girl," Russell would say.

And I'd reply, "I ain't."

We didn't have running water so Russell and Junior had to foot it to the public well every day, winter and summer, which was in the middle of the community and a heck of a chore to undertake. Thank God my sweet old dad said, "No girl can carry anythang dat heavy."

After the chores were done, we got permission to go play. I grabbed a cold biscuit off of the back of the stove. They were always there to snack on. Russell and Junior had already gone to the bottom of the hill to play.

"Thea-Thea, can I go play?"

"Yes, Baby Girl, be careful," she replied.

"Yes ma'am," I said as I ran out the door, down the steps, and down the hill. I was off to play until I heard my Thea-Thea calling my name over and over again . . . .

My very first stop was Ludie's house. She was sitting on the front porch, with a blanket around her frail frame.

"Hey, you," she would greet me as she hugged me close. "Where have you been all my life?" she would always say, swaying in her rocking chair as she hugged me tighter.

Ludie was an only child, and I seemed to be the only friend who took time with her. I would sit with her for a little while, and she would tell me what special places she had picked for me to hide, and then I would join the others. It was like she was playing all the games through me. She enjoyed telling me to *"Hurry, ClaraBy, and hide!"*

She would have sat on the porch during the day and strategically picked good hiding places for me to put my little frame. She was a master, as I seemed to never get caught. She was so thrilled when I would run as if I was a famous baseball player and touch the specific place that was the home base pole and be safe. She would squeal with delight.

"MY MAMA, YO MAMA, HANGING UP CLOTHES; MY MAMA HIT YO MAMA IN THE NOSE! ARE YOU READY? READY OR NOT, HERE I COME!

Everyone would run and hide behind anything they could find so as not to be called out by the one who was *It*. You didn't want to be discovered by *It* because then you had to be *It* and find everyone and call them out.

"Aww, man," you would say as *It* discovered you. You were out of the game then until everyone else came in safe or was caught.

5-10-15-20-25-30-35-40-45-50-55-60-65-70-75-80-85-90-95-100! ARE YOU READY? READY OR NOT, YOU SHALL BE CAUGHT!

Then, *It* would start the hunt! "1-2-3 for Olive behind Mr. Ben's car." Olive would come out slowly with her head down.

"Awww, man," she'd say." So on and so on.

This went on for as long as we could go, having *fun, fun, fun!* That's how I learned how to count by *fives*. I had it down pat. I could count to a hundred before I could hardly walk. I'm quite smart you know . . .

"Clara—*By*! Claraaa—*BY*!" Thea-Thea would be calling me from the front porch as it was approaching dusk.

"Clara—BY! Claraaaaa-BYYYYYY!"

The last part of my name always rang out louder than the first part as she bellowed it out.

Russell said, "Baby Girl . . . you hear Thea-Thea calling you—git home!" as he hit another basket in the makeshift hoop.

"YES, MA'AM, I'M COMING," I bellowed as I ran up the road, looking back longingly at the older kids still playing, including my two brothers, who could stay out longer than I could, as I was only five . . . or rather almost six years old.

By now, Ludie had gone in for the day. She went to bed quite early every evening.

What a crock of SHIT, I thought as I ran up the road. "Oops! Did I think the (*s*) word? You bet your sweet *Beeee-Hind* I did! You see us *chilluns* were pretty nosey during that time and I had heard that word quite often.

We were not allowed to stay in the same room as the grownups, but we certainly had our way of listening and looking in on them when they were having their private conversations—like about Mr. Tibbs going in Mr. Leonard's back door to *lay up* with Ms. Leonard, when he left to go to work in the mines. Seems like there was a lot of that going on in every coal camp in the county. They worked on different shifts, so Mr. Tibbs tipped in during the daytime before he went to work. He'd park his car at the foot of the church hill and sneak in Ms. Leonard's back door. I just thought he was going to visit.

Well, what else did you think I thought? I was just a smart five-almost-six-year-old nosey kid. My Big Mama would say, "Thea-Thea, ya had dat gal late in life, and she done been here be'fo, she too smart. She twice her age in mind. Be'fo, I tell ya! Hee, Heeee."

Chapter Four

MINDING MY OWN BUSINESS

I just happened to be minding my own business, in my own room, playing with my own dolls until one lazy evening, the ladies started to gather on our front porch for an evening of catching up.

Daddy was out back working in the garden, my brothers were out and about, and Big Sis was off with her *beau*.

I tiptoed down the steps and positioned myself by the window next to the front door, so as to be able to make a quick get away when necessary.

Ms. Katie, Ms. Nellie, Aunt Cellie, Ms. Noon and Ms. Francine came up the hill laughing and talking trash.

Thea-Thea asked, "What's so funny?"

And Aunt Cellie fell in a chair laughing so hard she could hardly talk. The other women were laughing just as hard. Aunt Cellie finally said, "Whee," as she tried to tell Thea-Thea what Ms. Katie had just said.

"Shit, Nellie, you know dat baby ain't Tom's."

Ms. Nellie laughed and said, "And what did I tell *huh?* I politely told huh to mind huh own damn business, 'cause I'm just like huh: *Mama's baby, Daddy's maybe . . . .*"

I didn't understand what Ms. Nellie meant, but they were all dying laughing, slapping their legs, throwing their heads back.

"Honey-child," Ms. Katie said, in her Deep-South drawl, 'ain't dat da God's truth, cause Elbert thanks Little Jim's his, and I just let him thank what he wants to, cause I hear he's got one down da road apiece too. So honey-child, I learned a long time ago, if ya can't take it, don't dish it out.... I stopped gittin' mad, and got even." They all laughed as she said to Thea-Thea, "Girl, ain't ya got nothin' to drink?"

Thea-Thea said, "Sho have. Come on, let's go to da kitchen." As they were getting up to go inside, Thea-Thea said, "Ya gossiping hens, one of these days ya gonna be talking bout somebody and she gonna be sitting right next to ya, and all *hell* gonna break loose.... Ya done heard bout reaping what ya sow, right?"

Ms. Francine said kindly, "I just don't thank Cecil would ever do anythang dat would hurt me, knowing we got dat sick child and all.... He so *dedicated*." Ms. Francine and Mr. Cecil were Ludie's parents.

Thea-Thea said under her breath, "Oh Lawd," as she reached for the screen door.

"Uh-Um," grunted Aunt Cellie, whose real name was Cecilia, getting up out of her chair and casting an eye at her sister, my Thea-Thea.

Thea-Thea looked back at her like she was remembering what Aunt Cellie had told her one breathless afternoon as she burst through the screen door....

I had heard her that day too; when I was, again, just minding my own business with my Sherlock Holmes ears open:

> "Ya can't breathe a word of dis," Aunt Cellie declared. "Promise, Thea-Thea, promise, ya have to take dis secret to yo grave!"
>
> Thea-Thea was standing with her hand over her mouth and a look of complete terror as she said, *"Ceeeeee-Leeeee, what's happened?!"*
>
> Knowing she had frightened Thea-Thea, Aunt Cellie said calmly, holding up her right pinky finger, "gimme yo pinky." Thea-Thea knew then that there was nothing wrong, well at least not in the family, as this was their childhood way of showing the trust they still carried.

"Soooooooooooo!" said Aunt Cellie, after the sisterly pinky-finger oath, "I had cooked a pot of pinto beans, and they was too much for just me, so I took some over to AnnaBelle's so she could have 'em for her kids," she said breathlessly, pacing the floor, wringing her hands.

Thea-Thea with a worried look on her face, screeched, "*And . . . and what Cellie?!*"

Aunt Cellie said, "*Well* . . . I walked upon da porch," she said, demonstrating, "and I knocked and opened da screen door, at da same time saying '*knock, knock!*'" She got very excited then, and said, "CHIIILD, *Cecil* had AnnaBelle in a bear hug behind da stove, gitting it ONNNN!"

Thea-Thea said, "Oh Lawd!"

Aunt Cellie flopped down in a kitchen chair and said disgustedly, "He gotta have a burn on his ass, cause he fell back on da stovepipe, as he bent over to pull up his pants!" Thea-Thea covered her mouth and groaned as Aunt Cellie continued. "AnnaBelle was hysterical. I was apologizing dat I hadn't knocked 'stead of busting in," Aunt Cellie screeched. But then I got mad—I mean I was ticked! The two of 'em standing there looking like they had done been caught wit they hand in da cookie jar.

"I started in on Cecil, 'YOU!' I screamed.

He ran like a scalded dog. AnnaBelle was standing there trembling . . . like a wilted flower, begging and pleading for me not to tell, saying she needed to buy some food, and Cecil was her undercover *sugar daddy,* and he was da way dat she had extra money to buy groceries . . . .

Well, as she cried and talked, I softened, and then in a state of shock, I tol' AnnaBelle dat her secret was safe wit me . . . . *but*" Aunt Cellie continued, "not till after I had done gave her a *piece a my mind!*"

My little heart was racing as Aunt Cellie stood up and leaned over the table to face Thea-Thea as she had faced Ms. AnnaBelle, saying, "Now I'm yo friend, but so is Francine. How could ya do dis to *her?* I screamed! AnnaBelle was crying uncontrollably, saying 'I'm sorry, I'm sorry.

"Well," said Aunt Cellie, now, dat's tween you and GOD. Just member dat when ya up in church sanging like an angel, looking out, and seeing Francine enjoying dat beautiful voice GOD done gave ya. Member just how *I'm sorry* ain't good enough . . . . And another thang,' I screamed, for *God's sake*, LOCK DA DAMN SCREEN DOOR! I left slamming da screen door hind me."

Aunt Cellie continued pacing the floor. "Now dis has done put me in a big bind! I got da chance to corner Cecil by hisself 'fore I got here. Da rat didn't have da nerve to go home—he was sitting on da Crow Pole, *on da Crow Pole of all places!* Da sorry sot didn't have da guts to face Francine.

"Well, I gave him a piece a my mind!" He looked like a sick puppy. I tol' him what a low down dirty dog he was. I tol' him, I'm only keeping my mouth shut cause of these women, not for *yo* sorry ass! Now ya know dis would kill Francine, and ya know AnnaBelle is desperate! Ya no-good SOB!

"He said, "sho, ya right, Cellie. I's got ta slow my roll," grinning and looking like a chessy cat.

"'Now ya done got me involved in dis ya no-good . . . ooooooooh, I could ring yo neck off myself! He sats there wit his hands in his pockets, jingling change saying, 'sho ya right, Cellie, sho ya right.'

"Oh, shut da . . . oooooooh. I felt so helplessly involved in dis mess. He was disgusting to look at. I turned to walk off and whirled around and *growled*: 'DON'T PULL DAT HOLIER THAN THOU AT DA FOOT OF DA CROSS, SHOUTING AND PRAISING B-S SUNDAY! DON'T! I'M GONNA STAND UP AND TELL DA WORLD BOUT YO SORRY GOOD-FOR-NOTHING . . . OOOOOOOOOOOOOOH!" Aunt Cellie screamed.

She breathed a sigh of relief as she said, *"Well,* needless to say, his grin faded, but I felt dirty, cause it seemed as if he was mo fraid a losing his upstanding repatation in da community than anythang else, so I fought to find something to say dat might reach down in his soul. I clinched my teeth and walked very close up to him, so dat he could smell my breath and know dat I meant business, as I growled, 'I might not be much, but I sho as hell ain't gonna play church, ya rotten SO 'N' SO! IT'S MEN LIKE YO SORRY BEHIND DAT MAKE ME WANNA PUKE!"

Thea-Thea seemed to snap back to reality as they were heading for the screen door, to come in the house. "Well," she said, "hee, hee . . . all I can say is, if I even *dream* dat Cal is having a nookie-fit, he can lay his Johnson on da chopping block, and *she's* in for da ass-whooping of her entire life, and I do mean dat goes for *anybody!*"

"I know what ya mean, Honey Child; ya can't trust nobody wit yo man, not even yo so-called friends," Ms. Nellie said. "Oooh, I don't mean y'all honcy, we's got too much in common." She kept on talking as they came into the house.

I took off upstairs as quickly and quietly as I could run so as not to be discovered eavesdropping, which I had down to a science.

Ms. Nellie continued, "Y'all know Tibbs is living danjously. I ain't never seen da beat. Tee gon' catch 'em yet, I feel it. They's gitting too bold wit they stuff."

"Ya sho right, girl," chided Aunt Cellie. "Mable tries to act so holy. Now dat's what gits my goat."

"ClaraBy?"

"Ma'am," I answered.

"Why ain't ya outside playing?"

"I am playing, Thea-Thea. I'm playing with my dolls. I don't want to go outside right now—it's too hot."

"Okay," she said.

Whooooo, that was close. I thought my goose was cooked, cause one thang's for certain and two thang's for sho: no kid was allowed to sit up under adults. When they showed up, you knew to disappear, and if you were a little slow in moving, you knew what the look on your mother's face meant without a word being spoken.

Man, I thought, *grownups lead a very exciting life.* There's always something going on, even though I had no clue what any of it meant. Well after all, I was only five-going-on-six years-old, you know, but I was pretty smart . . . so Ludie and my Big Mama told me.

Chapter Five

THE MARRIAGE (uggggh)

As I said before, my sister is getting married. Thank you, Lord. I will finally get the bed to myself.

There were two big double beds in Russell and Junior's room, so they had a bed to themselves, because my older brothers were long gone.

Me and Big Sis shared the other bedroom, with one double bed, and she hogged all the covers. All right already, I understand that I was a *long* time coming and she had had the room all to herself, but still . . . .

Our bedroom was over Thea-thea and Daddy's bed room and was a good spot for eavesdropping and eyeballing when the chance came. The boys' room had a vent also over the kitchen. There was not as much action going on in the kitchen, only gambling and cooking. Sometimes there was action but not nearly as much as what went on in the bedroom.

The kitchen was a large room, and Thea-Thea's pride and joy. She spent most of her time in there doing something. Daddy and my older brothers had built a meat house on the back porch, and it was full of salted-down meat and canned goods made fresh from the garden. It was always full, it seemed.

Thea-Thea spent a lot of time teaching Big Sis how to cook. She would tell her that the way to a man's heart is through his stomach. They laughed a lot as they tried different dishes.

Now, I was not at all feeling this big, tall, light-skinned, cursing-every-breath "Negro" that was coming to take my big sis away. Well, maybe not *away*, away, as they were only moving into a house just down the hill a stone's throw from my house . . . but . . . I didn't have to like it.

He had this haughty laugh, smoked like a train, and thought he knew everything. But Big Sis was totally smitten. She would whirl around and squeal whenever she saw him coming up the hill. Then when he'd come in the house, she act all prim and proper. They would sit on the porch and swing for hours, just looking at each other, holding hands.

What a crock, I thought. I had given up a lot of my playing time in the evening to spend more time with Ludie and then, off to the house I'd run cause *Mr. Man* was coming, and I wanted to keep an eye on him. I would go out back to the hog pen and talk to Little Red a little while until time for him to come. Little Red is the cutest pig I've ever seen and she was all mine. I fed her every day.

This day I was jumping rope in our front yard as Mr. Man was walking up the hill to our house. It had been discussed during one of Thea-Thea and Daddy's nightly talks how serious the relationship was becoming between Big Sis and Mr. Man, and this was an unannounced visit, so *What's up with that?* I thought. Well, as it turned out, he was coming to ask for Big Sis's hand in marriage:

"Hi, ClaraBy," he said.

"Hello, Mr. Man," I replied politely, as I continued to jump rope.

Daddy was sitting on the front porch with his feet propped up on the banisters. "HoneyBabe," he calls to my mama, "here he comes."

Thea-Thea handed Daddy a cold glass of lemonade, and said, "Oh dear, I thank I know what's on his mind." She nodded to him going into the house.

"Hello, ma'am, Mr. Cal," he said.

"Howdy, son," replied Daddy. "What brangs ya here this fine evening?"

"Well," Mr. Man stammered, "I ah . . . I ah . . . well . . . . You know I ah . . . I ah . . . ah."

"Un-huh," Daddy said. "Ya wanta ask me sumthin and ya don't know how, right?"

"Yes, yes, sir!" he said excitedly, scared to death. I want to ask for Evelyn's hand in marriage, sir . . . if you don't mind. I ah . . . work hard . . . . I'll be a good provider, and I love her and I ah . . . I ah . . ."

"Wooo, Woooo, son, slow down," Daddy said jokingly, "I knows ya nervous an' all."

"Yes, sir," said Mr. Man as he wiped the sweat from his brow with the back of his hand and took a deep breath.

One thing everybody knew about my daddy was that he did not play when it came to his family. Even the long arm of the law knew that, as they found out when a deputy came to arrest my older brother Oscar for a warrant his *ole lady* had taken out on him.

> Oscar and his ole lady Mamie had been fighting, and she had gone and taken a warrant out on him. The deputy came to serve it. Everything would have been all right if the deputy hadn't tried to show his manliness by trying to take Oscar in by brute force.
>
> Daddy and Oscar had just gotten home from work, so they were both still in their bankers. Daddy wanted to talk to Oscar about the fight before he went up the hollow where he and Mamie lived. They favored each other so much *without* the black dust on their faces, that nobody would've known which one was which behind the dust.
>
> The officer knocked on the door. Thea-Thea was startled as she asked, "Can I help ya, officer?"
>
> "Is Oscar Mickens here?" When Oscar answered, "Yes, sir," the officer told him he had a warrant for his arrest. Oscar tried to explain what had happened, but the officer wasn't interested, so he grabbed Oscar by the arm pulling his handcuffs out. Oscar was still trying to explain when he pulled his billy club and hit Oscar upside the head with it.

Needless to say, Daddy went ape on him. He grabbed the first thing he saw, which was the old iron skillet that always sat on the stove, and slammed the officer over his head with it.

Thea-Thea grabbed Daddy's arm as the officer staggered backward. We were all screaming—Big Sis, Thea-Thea, Junior, Russell, and me. The boys were trying to calm Daddy down. Thea-Thea and Big Sis were trying to help the officer, who was bleeding.

Finally, after what seemed forever, the officer seemed to calm down to the point of reason. "I'm puttin' ya both under arrest. Now we can do this peaceably—it's yo choice."

Thea-Thea was crying, saying, "Please don't take 'em to jail, mister, *please!*"

The officer said, "I'm gonna radio for help."

"No, no, officer, they go peaceably," screeched Thea-Thea.

Everybody was scared to death—the buzz was that they would be beaten while in jail, or worse.

Daddy wouldn't bow though. He told the officer, "I'll go quiet, but ya don't understan', nobody hits my chillun, *nobody.*"

Thea-Thea bandaged Oscar's head. The officer handcuffed both of them, put his bloody hat back on his head, opened the back door of the police car, and Daddy and Oscar got in quietly.

We were all scared to death. I didn't understand it at all, so I was hysterical as my daddy was being taken away. I cried uncontrollably. Daddy tried to calm me down, but I couldn't help it. I held on to his leg until Thea-Thea had to pry me loose.

Mamie ended up dropping the warrant on Oscar, but he and Daddy had to spend a few days in jail. Mr. Mitch, the boss at the mines, had to bail them out in time to make the Monday morning shift.

Daddy said, "I's got to toe da line now cause I'm on probation for a year." He told Thea-Thea that he never had respect for a white man as he did for Mr. Mitch, and that he owed him a lot of gratitude. "I's don know what strangs he had to pull to git us out, but I's sho is glad he had some." Daddy said, "'Sides y'all, HoneyBabe, I'd die for dat man. Yep," he said, "I respect 'em just dat much."

Daddy reassured Mr. Man that he understood him being nervous by saying, "Don't be nervous, son, I felt da same way bout asking HoneyBabe's mama *anythang*.... So ya wanta marry my daughter?" he said.

"Yes, sir," said Mr. Man.

"Well, Daddy said, I's got one rule an one rule only."

I jumped a little closer to the steps as Daddy leaned over to him and spoke slowly. "Son, I done raised her . . . and did a damn good job if I say so myself, . . . so she don't need no daddy, . . . and she ain't yo servant . . . . Slavery over, right?"

"Yess, sssirrrrr," Mr. Man stuttered.

"Sooo," continued Daddy. "If ya wanta keep on breathing God's great air, ya had better not never lay a hand on her, understand?"

"Yessss, sir, I, I, I understand, Mr. Mickens. I love Evelyn, and I would never hurt her. I'll take real good care of her. I promise!" Mr. Man stammered.

Daddy said quietly, "Ya do dat, son, ya do dat," as he started rocking and smoking his pipe.

Mr. Man said, "Well, sir, I'll be going now, got to get up early in the morning."

And he flew! He was so glad to get away from the wrath of the future father-in-law. Heeee, heeee, I loved it.

Git him, Daddy, I thought. I was proud of my daddy. *Now what's next, Mr. Man, bring it on*! I started jumping red-hot pepper, as fast as I could . . . . Big Sis was upstairs more than likely praying that daddy wouldn't go off on Mr. Man.

* * *

"Who in da hell gits married in Febarary!" said Ms. Nellie. "He already showing signs of being pussy-whooped. Honey-child, she done smothered him," she carried on, roaring with laughter.

Big Sis wanted to get married on her birthday, which happened to be on a Sunday, in the heart of winter, the coldest month of the year, and I was not even invited to the ceremony. This was held in *my* house, in the front room, which was my Thea-Thea and Daddy's bedroom! Now you think of that! Me, the baby of the family, my sister getting married, and I had to peep through the window . . . as Russell and Junior had the vent occupied and wouldn't budge an inch.

But I was determined not to miss the ceremony as this was my very first. So I headed down the steps from my bedroom, through the kitchen, out the back door, around the house and up the front steps to peep through the window

She's my sister! I thought *what do they know?* They never heard the secret talks we had at night. She would tell me stories about her school days. She said she always only wanted to be a wife and mother, with a big house, a white picket fence and lots of kids.

She would say, "When you get older, I'm gonna tell you everything you should know about being a woman." She had quit school in the ninth grade and had gone to work for a rich white couple about five miles down the road. "You know, Baby Girl," she said, "I almost feel like you're my child." Then we'd cuddle and fall asleep. Sometimes, she would read to me until I fell asleep.

"I'm not gonna cry. I'm not gonna cry," I kept repeating. It was *me and my Big Sis,* not this dummy she was marrying. I was deeply hurt . . . I . . . I . . . I was losing my sis . . . my bed would be empty now. I thought I was going to be happy having the bed to myself, but now that it was really happening, I was feeling the loss.

The Reverend, his wife, Daddy, Thea-Thea, my sister, Mr. Man, and his parents—Mr. and Ms. Wiley—were the only ones present. I learned that day that Mr. Man's name was Napoleon Wiley. Big Sis was all dressed in white. I was thinking to myself, s*he looks like an angel*. Mr. Man kissed her. *Uggggggggghhhh,* I thought.

Chapter Six

MR. MAN'S FAMILY

Well, life goes on, and Mr. Man is welcomed into the family. But still, I wasn't feeling him at all, but Thea-Thea and Daddy thought the world of him.

He worked in the same mine as my daddy; only he had been switched to the evening shift while my daddy worked on the day shift. So Daddy was coming when he was going, and I would then go to his house to see my big Sis.

"Did I say *Big* Sis, well, that was an understatement: all of a sudden, she is getting fat all over. *My* sister, my one and only sister! The one who was built like a brick house before she married this dummy, with a waistline you could almost get both hands around, "hips like Lone Ranger's horse HI-HO Silver Away," and beautiful big brown legs. Now, she looked like she had swallowed something and it was growing. She grew and grew. I didn't know exactly what was wrong. I just thought she ate too much of that good cooking she had learned to do.

Besides, I had started school and no longer had time to spend with her every day, so I thought, *Well, stufff happens, I guess.* After all, I was only a smart, nosey, singing, dancing, shouting, been-here-before-so-I've-been-told, six-year-old.

Big Sis and Mr. Man came up to the house every Sunday evening. After dinner, everyone went to the front porch. One spring evening, Mr. Man asked Daddy to tell him about their lives down south.

Mr. Man's parents lived in the next camp above ours, where one of my other best friends, Janice lived. Daddy and Mr. Man's parents were all raised in the same area down south and ended up in the same community up here as adults. They were the best of friends, and though Mr. Wiley was a homebody, they often visited each other to catch up and to reminisce. Sitting on the front porch this fine Sunday evening, Daddy began telling Mr. Man about life down south.

"Yo mama, as a young thang, was a very bright, damn-near-white-skinned woman, wit brownish blonde hair. She coulda easily passed for white, but ya could tell when ya got close to her dat she had heavy *Negro* blood . . . if ya knowed what to look for, especially da nose . . . and her hair was a dead giveaway if she didn't wet it down.

"White folk never paid 'tention to such though, so lessen they knowed ya and yo folks, ya could git way wit it." Daddy said, "Well, what can I say? She was bo'n in Alabamie and dat says it all. She was da grandchild of a slave family who still worked on da same farm, when she met George. Da plantations weren't dat far apart. We played together all da time when we got da chance. *Passing* was done by a lota colored folks back den, yep, lota folks.

"Ya know, yo folks had to run away to be together, 'cause yo mama looked too white, and yo daddy had been beat up by four white boys down by da creek where he and yo mama was sitting on da banks, coating one day."

"Yeah," Mr. Man said. "Daddy told me and Cindy that he had to hide away and escape or be killed. He said they told him that if they saw them together again, they'd kill him. Even though they knew Mama was Negro—because one of the boys' families owned the farm Gran-maw worked on."

Daddy said, "Yep, dat's right, son. HoneyBabe, I believe she was probly gon' to be da apple of one of dem boys' eye, if'n not all of 'em. Ya know what I mean?"

Which I didn't understand naturally, but it sure sounded delicious.

Thea-Thea replied, "Now ya *know* I know what ya mean!"

Mr. Man said that his grandfather had snuck his daddy out of town that same night. They hid him under a haystack in the back of a neighbor's old pickup truck and drove him to the next town, gave him clean clothes in a old feed sack, and some money to catch the next bus as far away as he could get.

He said, "Daddy told us that he was let out of the truck as close to the bus terminal as possible, so if there was any question about where he was, his family could simply say they didn't know. He stayed hid all night, not sleeping, waiting for the bus terminal to open."

Mr. Man said, "Daddy told me, Son, I was looked at by all da white folk at dat little terminal as if I's was some kinda disease or sumthin'. They ask me where I was headed. I tol' em I was headed up north to my mama's sister, to look for work. Where ya coming from, boy?" they asked. I tol' em, I's from 'Bama, sir; I don't got no paper to show who I is." So I played da dumb-as—dirt role as best I could, and I's just prayed to da good Lawd dat I could git by, and thanks be to God, I made it here."

Mr. Man continued, "Daddy said he wasn't leaving without Mama. He was afraid of what might happen to her. So my Gran-maw and others ladies had secretly begged up enough money for Mama that night, and the next morning she was driven to the bus terminal."

Mr. Man laughed as he said, "By her being darn near white, and young as she was, she could pass, and she did by sitting in the third seat behind the bus driver. She had been dressed up to appear white in a nice dress, gloves, bonnet and shoes. Her suitcase wasn't the best, but it could pass. She had changed her name, so if anybody asked, she would tell them she was Susan Chambers from Mobile, Alabama, going to Chicago for summer vacation. Ha, ha, ha, Mama said she was so proper, she almost fooled herself! She thought to herself, *I just might pull this white thang off.*"

"Daddy said he got as far in the back of the bus as he could so as not to be seen looking at Mama. He said, 'She was da prettiest thang on dat bus, and she is all mines." Mr. Man went on to say, "Daddy said 'Chilluns, I was busting inside wit pride, scared to death, but wanting to shout it to da world."

Mr. Man seemed to enjoy telling how his parents had done such a brave thing to be together for love.

I was lying on the porch on my belly, with my face in my hands, listening intently. My little imagination was running away with the scenes going through my mind. *This love thing seems to be something*, I thought. Ludie was all the time telling me about how Jesus *loved* us so much that he died for us all. Now, I thought, *That's some loving there.*

Mr. Man said his mama had told him and his sister how she had gone into the department store across from the bus terminal and bought the cheapest and darkest makeup available, which was not very dark at all, but she said she had to make it work. Once they arrived in the town they were going to, she would mix it with flour that she had browned on the stove. "Daddy said it took some doing, but they finally made it by using their *mother wit*. He said, 'Boy, using the old noggin will git ya through most anythang ya sat yo mind to. Yes indeed, son, yes indeed.' So they ended up in West (by God) Virginia, because the money had run out."

Thea-Thea spoke up and said, "Ya know, chilluns, God knows already where ya gonna end up at, He just lets ya to go through thangs so dat ya 'preciate what He got in stow for ya. Dat's why I trust Him." Looking as if her mind was far away, she say again, "Yes, sir, dat's why I trust Him."

My daddy said that he was shocked to see ole George Wiley. They couldn't believe they were in the same place. "Uhm, uhm, uhm, I was sho glad to see him, Daddy said. We hugged and cried, as I tol' him how *I* ended up here."

Mr. Man said, "Mama often laughs about how she got over on the bus drivers and all the rest of them *uppity* white folks on the buses. She said they talked about their maids and other *nigras* they still somewhat *owned*, even though slavery was over. She pretended to sleep a lot and watch the scenery, never joining in their conversations, scared she might give herself away. When changing buses, she was careful to make herself busy by reading or something, with her head down when Daddy passed her. He said he always made sure that he went straight to the back of each bus without question, his eyes straight ahead."

Mr. Man's mama, Ms. Wiley, whose real name is Lilly Mae, not (Susan Chambers), was a little on the heavy side, and her long, wavy, brownish-blonde hair, when combed out, was almost to her waist. She was very jolly and a homebody; she seemed to always be happy. She seemed perfectly content to stay at home. She said she didn't go many places, because she didn't want nobody questioning Mr. Wiley about her.

She had a #3-tub behind, and so did his sister Cindy. They were well-endowed. That must be a Negro trait or something, cause most of the women in the camp were big hipped and bow legged. Big hips, pretty big lips and bow legs. Thea-Thea said that Reverend Berry said that it was an African heritage thing, having to carry heavy things on their heads made their back sides strong. So I started practicing in my room with books on my head, cause I wanted those big hips, I already had the lips and bow legs.

Mr. Man's sister had moved to the city of Detroit with her husband who now worked for one of the big car factories.

His daddy, Mr. Wiley, was part Indian, Negro, white, you name it, he looked it. He had a medium complexion with very straight, coal black hair and high cheek bones, teeth as white as the driven snow, made even whiter when he smiled under that black mustache. He was a handsome man, a coal miner, and another staunch union man who didn't take no junk.

He and my daddy were a lot alike. Their childhoods were very similar, and now that they were men, you had better treat them like one—no matter what color you were.

Chapter Seven

WHAT THE WORLD? WHAT THE WORLD!

Well, call me dumb, but I woke up one morning, with Thea-Thea shouting, "It's a girl! It's a girl!"

"What the world? What the world! I thought as I jumped out of bed and ran downstairs to see what the ruckus was about.

"ClaraBy! ClaraBy!" she screamed. "We got a baby girl!" Thea-Thea had been down to Big Sis's practically all night after Mr. Man came to tell her excitedly that, "It was time . . . ." She had come back home to get me and to tell Daddy, Junior, and Russell the good news.

She bent down on one knee and informed me at my level that I was an aunt now. I thought, *What the world?—an ant?*

She said, "Ya know—like yo *Aunt* Cellie."

I rubbed my still sleepy eyes, "Sooo . . . ?"

"Come on, child!" she exclaims, "Let's go to yo sister's and see da new baby."

"NEW BABY! What new baby!?"

She said, laughing, "Da stork done brought a beautiful baby girl and left her wit yo sister."

"What's a stork?"

Thea-Thea said, "Oh, it's a big bird, wit a big mouth to carry babies in."

"Oooh," I said, somewhat puzzled. Well. I was flabbergasted and a little bit excited as she put shoes on my feet with no socks and threw a coat over my shoulders.

Thank God it wasn't that cold, because it *was* November! Anyway, out the door and down the hill to Big Sis's house we ran. And, low and behold, there it was, *a little gremlin!* I thought. It was all wrinkly and squirming and screeching.

I said, "Thea-Thea, what is it?"

She said, "It's yo sister's baby, like you was when you was a baby, and she's gonna grow just like ya."

"Oooh," I said. Still puzzled, but I let it be, mumbling, "I hope I didn't look like that!"

It was Saturday morning, and the men were beginning to gather at their usual place, the Crow Pole. The first man there was always the one who started the fires in the two big barrels they had to keep warm by.

Mr. Man—which was the name I had given him, as I was not on a first-name basis with him as yet—came home from the store with a box of cigars, which he passed out proudly. All of the men were slapping him on his back and shaking his hand, which I didn't understand: *why was* he *getting so much attention*? My sister was lying in there looking like she was on her last leg, and he was getting cheered on as if he had hit the numbers for some big money or something. I thought the BIG BIRD had done the work; what in the world did Mr. Man do?

Well, being nosy as I was, I asked, "Thea-Thea, what did Mr. Man do that everybody is shaking his hand and patting him on the back?"

Thea-Thea said, "Oh, child, he had a lot to do wit da baby gitting here. He had to show da stork da right house, so as not to leave da baby in da wrong place."

"Ooooh," I said.

The women were guarding my sister, making sure she did not move a muscle. Old lady Thomas throwing out instructions of what she couldn't do. She could do *nothing*, and I do mean *nothing*, for a whole entire month. WHAT THE WORLD! WHAT THE WORLD! Ms. Thomas told her, as she was leaving, gathering her stuff she had brought with her that she could not even stick her head out the door.

I asked Big Sis, "Why did this make you so sick if the stork brought the baby?"

She said, taking my hand in hers, "I had to help the stork bring the baby here from Babyland, and I'm tired." She slowly got up, and Thea-Thea helped her, to use the slop jar. Then she said, "Turn your head, and keep it turned."

"Okay," I said.

She said, "You'll understand it later in life, just as I promised you, but now is not the time to tell you. Just know that I am very happy."

Then I noticed, as she returned to get in the bed, that she was not fat anymore, maybe a little puffy, but not fat. *Hummm*, I thought, *oh well* . . . . "Thea-Thea, can I go tell Ludie about the baby?"

"You sho can, child. Tell ev'rybody about my first grandchild! Oh my, my, my . . ." she was saying lovingly as she looked at the tiny bundle. I ran as fast as I could to tell Ludie.

Chapter Eight

THE CROW POLE

The Crow Pole was made of split trees nailed to tree stumps. The men had cut down two big trees some years ago that stood outside the fence, as the limbs had hung way over in the Sidney's yard, making them a nuisance. The men made a long bench by splitting the trees in half and smoothing out the rough parts, nailing the halves to stumps so they wouldn't have to stand all day.

Pearlie was the Sidney's daughter and one of my best friends. On Saturdays, after I had finished my chores, I would often go straight to Pearlie's. Heee, heeeee, she was getting good at eavesdropping too, although I was the master. A fence divided the Crow Pole and the Sidney's yard, so it was easy to act like you were busy at play and not just being a nosy kid. It was a good hiding place for hide-n-seek until Olive got a big ole splinter in her hand and started squalling and got us all caught by the other kid playing *It*.

Some men sat on the bench, the rest of them stood with one foot resting on the bench to the sides and in back of the men sitting down.

A coal miner's stance—or *stand*—is very noticeable. I learned later in life that the stand represented the hard work they had to do on their knees with their backs in a strain as they shoveled and loaded the coal cars. Daddy said, "Ya can almost always tell a coal miner by da way he stands when he's deep in conversation. It helps take the weight off yo back."

Yes I had noticed that, especially the older miner with the back problem, who used one leg for support during a long conversation with one in front of the other with a little bend to the back, and often shifting from one leg to the other.

The Crow Pole started to get crowded with the community men, and even some from other coal camps. On the weekends, they gathered there and laughed and lied all day, especially on off-paydays.

Mr. Tucker was upset because he had missed the numbers the day before. He said, "I's been playing dat dag-gon' thang ever' day, I tell ya, ever' day and da day I miss playing, dat sapsucker, it comes out. Hot damn, hot damn!" he said, shaking his head in disbelief.

All the men were agreeing with him, some saying they had missed it by one number, when Mr. Foster shouted, "Here he comes!"

It was Mr. Tibbs. He drove a big blue Chevrolet, and in the trunk, he had a tub full of bottles of beer, cold on ice, twenty-five cents a piece. The men were ready now to really start telling their tall tales.

Money was low, but spirits were high as they shared with the have-nots. Everybody had their fair share—including Mr. Tibbs, who drank up any profit he could have made.

My daddy started by telling the story of how he came to be here in West Virginia. He said he was working on the railroad as the head cook down South, way back up in the woods. One day, the boss (a white man) came to the cook car and told him that he wanted some corn bread for supper.

Daddy said, "I tol' em, I says, 'Mr. Sullen, there ain't no clean water left to make no co'n bread.' I tol' em. But nooo . . . he turns and says all mad like, "There had better be some co'n bread when I come back to eat! I want dat damn bread!"

"Well," Daddy said, "I had no choice but to make da bread wit da dish water. It didn't turn out good at all, hard as a rock. Da bastard knowed we was low on supplies, but he had to show me his balls was bigger than mines, I guess. Da truck was due in da mo'nin."

Daddy continued by saying, "Ole man Charlie, who was da other cook, had used da last of da clean dranking water for fresh lemonade for da sorry sots. There was fo' of 'em, and they tried to eat up everythang from da other men. Ya couldn't never satisfy 'em, it seemed. Da rest of da men et whats-so-never was left after da big wheels et."

Daddy said, "Well, me and Charlie was good at making a meal out of nothin', but we couldn't make water, dat's fo' sho'. We had made beef stew for da whole crew and some biscuits, so now we was waiting on da supply truck to come.

"Charlie was worried and asked me, "Cal, what we's gon' do now?"

Daddy said, "I tol' Charlie, there ain't no choice but to make it wit da dish water". Charlie shouted, "Dish water? Heee, Heeeee, now Cal, ya know dang well dat ain't gon work."

"Well, dat's what I'm gon' do," Daddy said, "He'll git his co'n bread.

"So when da bosses comes in to eat, laughing and talking, I brangs da kettle of beef stew and da co'n bread to da table, wit a big dipper spoon, and sat em on da table. Charlie had done already put da biscuits and lemonade out.

"Now I's been cooking all my life, 'specially if I wanna eat, so I knows da bread ain't no prize, but he wanted it and he got it." Daddy said, "Da boss man picked up da bread, and said, *What da hell is this?*"

"I says, all meek an' mild like, 'Dat yo co'n bread, suh. I did da best I could wit what I had to work wit. I tol ya there weren't no clean water."

You could tell by the tone of Daddy's voice that he was reliving the incident as he said, demonstrating, "Dat dirty bastard stood up and throwed dat pan of bread—BAM!—upside my head. I staggered back a little, mostly 'cause I was mo' su'prised than I was hurt."

All of the men were listening intently, not saying a word; it seemed as if they all could see the scene.

Daddy said, "I was pissed, but I didn't say a mumbling word. He continued, saying, 'Aaahhh . . . .' He marched back and fo'th, back and fo'th, cussing and carrying on. One of da men says to him, 'Let it go, Sul, let it go, eat da damn biscuits! Ya know da truck ain't run yet!'

"Ya could see da sadness in they eyes, but none of 'em said nothin', they all just started gitting da food and talking to each other 'bout da day.

"Finally, Sullen sot down, still mumbling, but nobody paid him no mind. I gathered myself and went to da stove, and started wiping wit all my might to calm down. Charlie, just stood there, looking at 'em., and Sullen said, 'What ya looking at, Charlie?' And Charlie said low, but loud 'nough for 'em to hear, 'Nun-thin' much, suh, nun-thin' much,' as he turned round to da pots and pans and started washin' 'em."

Daddy sits back down on the bench, sighing real deep, "I ain't one to cry, I can't tell ya da last time I did. But I tell ya true, I cried after dem men left dat cook car. I cried, I tell ya. Charlie never said a word, he just started humming dat ole Negro spiritual, 'Nobody knows . . . da trouble I see . . . nobody knows my sorrow . . .' I soon got calm 'nough to thank. I tol' Charlie, I says, 'Charlie, I's got to go!'

"Charlie says, real low, 'I know, Cal, I know.'

"I kept on talking calmly, 'I's just as much man as he is, and mo' from what I's seen 'em pull out in da woods where we go do our bis-niss.' Then, it seems like I was gonna bust open. I screamed, 'No man, I mean *no man* lays a hand on me and gets 'way wit it! I don't have to take dis shit, and I don't 'tend to take it!' I slammed my fist down on da table, rattling da dishes. 'I hate to leave Charlie, but I'm gone 'fore I have to kill da SOB.'

"So I packed my little belongings, and left walking. I walked da other way where ever' body stayed, so's not to be seen leavin'.

"Well, Charlie thought I had done left, but I hid in da woods. Ya see, da sapsucker had some kinda problem, so ever' evening after supper 'tween seven and eight o'clock, he had da runs. Well," Daddy said, "I was waitin' fo' em." Daddy said boldly, *"I shot 'em in his ass and don't know if da SOB lived or died, 'cause I hauled ass!"*

The men died laughing . . . Some of them were bent over, they were laughing so hard; some of them were leaning against the fence for support as they laughed.

Catching his breath, Mr. Tibbs said, "Calvin, ya mean to tell me ya shot da man in his ass?"

"Yep, sho' did!" Daddy said proudly.

The men were still laughing when Mr. Tibbs, barely able to talk, said, "They's prob'ly still looking fo' yo black ass!"

They roared with laughter again . . . some holding their sides, some slapping their legs, some acting the scene out, "CA-PA-YAL!" howling with laughter.

"Whee . . ." they said, after calming down a bit.

Chapter Nine

HoneyBabe

Daddy continued to tell them how he met his HoneyBabe. "I left da Deep South running and went to No'f Car'li-ne. Dat's where I met my sweetheart," he said, hitting his pipe on the heel of his shoe.

"She was a pretty, young thang. She was da baby of six chilluns. Her other sisters and brothers had done left home when they came of age. Some of da girls got married. Da boys just left looking for work, sending back what little money they could to *Big Mama*, to help her out.

"She had to quit school when she was in da fo'th grade to help her mother run da boarding house," he said. "She was growing into a beautiful young thang of fifteen or so.

"Well, dat's where I ended up renting a room at da boarding house. Ever' evening at suppertime, Delores helped her mother set da table and serve da food. There was seven men living in da big boarding house. I was da youngest," he said. "We all worked on da road dat was coming through. All of 'em was eyeing her," he said, "but I had made it clear dat she was gon' to be mines."

So ever' payday, I started leaving her a little donation under my plate, after thanking her on da meal. She never said much, but 'Thank ya, suh. Well, I was quite older than her, I had her by quite a few years, but da other old codgers was much older."

"I made sho dat I kep' in Big Mama's good graces, 'cause she didn't play. She let it be knowed right off da bat: 'Da first SOB dat 'proaches my baby won't wake up da next morning, 'cause I'm gonna poison his ass.' Heee, heeee! Well, we knowed she packed a

.45 in her hussy bag under her apron. All dem hungry dogs knowed she meant it, so they kept they cool. But me, I was determined to win her over.

"Well, I finally got da nerve to 'proach Big Mama." Daddy said, "I asked her like this, 'Big Mama,' I said softly, 'ah . . . I . . . ah, well, I ah . . .'

"She said, 'Well, out wit it, what da hell do ya want?'

"I replied, swallowing real hard, 'Big Mama, I's scared ya might get mad.'

"She said, 'No I won't get mad, but it better be good.'

"'Well,' I said, 'I's would like to ask Delores if she would . . . ahh . . . only wit yo permission . . . . Ya know, I wouldn't say a word to her if ya say so, but I would . . . ahh . . . I would . . .'

"'Oh boy, spit it out, ya wanta *coat* my baby?'

"'Well, not 'xactly . . . I don know if'n she wants me to.'

"'Well,' Big Mama said, 'I'll ask her, an if she says yes, den ya can sit wit her one hour a week, in da front room, wit me sitting right 'cross from ya, looking ya straight in da eye!'

"'Yes, ma'am, yes, ma'am, dat's fine wit me!' I says, bowing and backing out da room at da same time. 'Thank ya, ma'am!' Ya talking 'bout kissing ass—man, I was kissing ass dat day."

The men all fell out laughing again.

"Well," Daddy continued, "it started from there and grew into a little coat-ship. Then it growed into a very nice little romance. We got married when she turned seventeen. 'Spite Big Mama's hard outer shell, she was very religious, and ya could hear her praying in da wee hours of da night. I thank da men thought she had some kind of voo-doo powers, but I knowed she was a good woman at heart—she just had to have dat hard outer shell for da world to git by.

"Well, I heard about da mines in Kentucky and another state called West-by-God-Virgi-ne. A lot of da men was headed dis way. So dat's how we ended up here, and we's been here ever since."

Mr. Anderson said, "Cal, ya one lucky man, cause it seems like ya 'scaped wit yo life to end up in another tough situation, 'cause I know Big Mama don't play."

Their laughter could be heard from a distance.

Daddy said through laughter, "Ya got dat right!"

Mr. G-Baby said, "Sho' ya right, but dat sorry sot deserved it. I betcha his runs stopped."

"Haaaa, haaaaaa," they all laughed.

Then Mr. G-Baby would tell his "World War" story. This went on all day, until the men would begin to drift off to their different homes to get ready for their usual night of activity. Then the only sound you heard was the children playing. People were sitting out on their porches rocking and talking. When it's a slow weekend and money is low, the women would always make sure there was something to do, as they would pool their assets and just do something fun. There were quiet times, but never dull.

Chapter Ten

COAL MINER'S TALK

Mr. Man, Big Sis, and the baby came to the house every chance they got, sitting on the front porch with Daddy, talking about the mines.

From time to time, my older brothers would come—as often as they were allowed, that is, as their mates never visited.

Daddy would let Russell, Junior, and I set on the porch with them, listening to them talking. It was interesting to me how they said they had to crawl around in the mines, hoping the top wouldn't fall. Daddy said he could hear the roof cracking above his head. He and my brothers were *pinners;* they would put up roof bolts to hold the top up.

My brother Oscar asked Daddy. "Ole Man, do you think that top is safe enough?"

Daddy replied, "Son, it's 'bout as safe as ya make it."

"Yeah, I guess you right, 'bout that," Oscar replied.

Daddy said, "Boys, ya gotta look out for yo own safety, so don't slack on yo job, and make sho' dat da man working wit ya ain't slacking fo' sho'. I hate to say it, but I's 'fraid somethin' gonna happen one of these days. Yep, sumthin bad."

Mr. Man was called a *loader*. He loaded the *buggy*, or shuttle car. Mr. Man said, "You know, the coal is back-breaking low. Low coal, low, low coal. "It ain't that the work is so terribly hard," he said, 'cause it's a fair living and 'bout the only decent job around for a black man, but you just in a strain all the time, and the darkness makes it more dangerous."

Frank said with a sadness, "Man, the dust is so thick, and you breathing it in all the time . . . can't be good. Every man that comes out looks the same, covered black with dust. You can't tell whose face is behind the dust."

Daddy said, "Boys, somethin' gotta be done 'bout da dust. Don't, it's gonna kill us all."

They stopped talking for a while and let their minds wonder about the unknown.

Listening to them talk made me respect Mr. Man more and more. I was beginning to *feel* him, just a little. I'm a hard nut to crack.

The men continued long into the evening talking about the mines.

Big Sis and Thea-Thea headed to the kitchen to make a snack and drinks. me and the boys off to our room. Sometimes, they would be joined by other miners for an evening of "coal mining talk." It was their life . . . and their love.

Chapter Eleven

My Little Boo

The little gremlin, had turned into the cutest little thing you ever saw. Mr. Man named her Paula, She was so much fun now. Thea-Thea would let me hold her. She would be looking at me and smiling, and I would just melt. But then, she'd get all red in the face, frowning and grunting

I screamed, "Oohhhh, Thea-Thea, she stinks! She just let a big POOT, and I think she has lost her manners!" That was the only thing I didn't like about this live, moving doll. My baby dolls didn't do that. This one was broke, I thought.

Thea-Thea said, "Baby Girl, she not a play thang; she real! She does ever'thang you do."

"I know, but why so much, and, and why . . . ?"

"Oh, child," Thea-Thea would say, "just go git me a diaper."

"Yes, ma'am."

I was glad to give her back to Thea-Thea, who was looking at her and saying some mumble-jumble words, "coooch-coooch, coo, coooch-coooch coo." The little gremlin got *all* of the attention when she was around.

My daddy had a tune that he had sung to all his chilluns, and he said he would do the same with his grans. *"Toooly-toooly-tooo-ly, toooly-toooly-tooo, tooly-toooly-toooly, tooo, toooly, toooly-toooooo!"* He was standing over Thea-Thea singing as she changed the poopy diaper, as if it was the greatest feat in the world. Poop was all over her little butt.

Thea-Thea cleaned it perfectly and said, "Here, Baby Girl, go put it in da bucket by da stove; ya know, da one wit da water in it."

"EeeeeeGaggg," I carried it as if it was dynamite with my nose up in the air.

Thea-Thea was saying as she raised Paula in the air, "Dat's yo bucket! Yes it is, yes it is. Maw-Maw got ya all fixed up! Yes I do, yes I do."

They loved little Paula with a passion, and so did I . . . when she wasn't *POOTING!*

Chapter Twelve

COMMUNITIES

Everybody raised gardens and had hogs and chickens. So most of the children didn't know when there was no money, 'cause our bellies were full . . . except for Sarah and J. J.—they ate at our table quite often. Thea-Thea always made sure she had extra for unexpected *and expected* "show-ups."

The only thing that seemed to not be doing so well, was the well, which you had to prime and prime and prime to get water.

One evening, when the boys came back with only half buckets of water, Daddy said, "Da company is finding another way to git water. They gon' try to put water in each house. Now, dat's gonna take some time, but they's working on it. I sho' hope so, yes sir, I sho' do."

Thank God for rain. We kept big barrels out back, which would fill up with rainwater that was used for bathing and washing when necessary. There was nothing like fresh rainwater to wash your hair in. I think that was a trait of the community—when it rained, all the women and girls got their hair washed. It felt so soft!

Our gardens were plentiful, and Big Mama would come all the way from Virginia on the big Trailways bus to help can the food. They canned everything.

Big Mama had moved from North Carolina some years back. She now lived with Thea-Thea's sister Aunt Idella.

We were all "po," but the kids didn't know, 'cause most of our parents made us immune to it. No matter how bad things were, we never knew it. But compared to J. J. and Sarah, we felt rich, because they seemed *sooo* poor. We all felt sorry for them. They never seemed to have much of anything! But everyone in the community helped out by giving them some hand-me-downs and keeping them fed.

There seemed to be at least one or two people at our table at mealtime every other day that wasn't a family member: Russell's best friend Shelby one day, Junior's best friend Jerry—who was a white boy—one day or another. J. J. and Sarah . . . well, often. Junior's friend Jerry lived in the *first white camp* where the "big dogs" over the mines here and there lived. It was a beautifully, manicured camp located on the right side as you crossed the bridge coming up the hollow. This section separated the other communities. The big house that sat off to it self was where Jerry lived with his family. His father was the superintendent of the coal mines.

Just past the big house, was a little knoll leading up to the railroad tracks and past the tracks was the big company store and the adjoining doctor's office. To the left of the store was the post office, and down in a little gulley was the one-room school for the little colored kids, first through fourth grades.

A little farther up the dirt road stood what was called a *tipple where the coal taken from the mines was dumped and separated from slate to be loaded into the big empty coal cars that the train brought in. It* loomed over the first white camp where the coal miners and their families lived.

Separating the tipple from the community was the dirt road and a bridge to cross over the creek.

All of the company houses in each community looked the same. They were two-family houses, with four rooms on each side, and two outside toilets—one for each family—with a public well somewhere in each community. Then there was a large, longhouse called a boarding house at the end of the row of houses on the left side, where the foreign workers lived.

Daddy said, "Ole man Bimp brought some Hungarian galosh or somethin' to work, and man, HoneyBabe, it was good ev'n cold. They sho' can cook."

Each community where the coal miners worked was homey and had the feeling of family. The manicured section seemed artificial and aloof, quiet and mysterious. Children were seldom seen outside playing . . . well, at least we never saw them.

There was about a quarter mile of nothing but woods on one side, a slate dump that smoldered all of the time, the dirt road, the creek, and the railroad leading to the next camp, which was the *first black camp,* where I lived.

There were eight double houses, four on each side, with a dirt road down the middle. Each side had its own outside toilet. Now, we didn't live down in the bottom. Our house was located up on a hill above the community. We had four, large rooms. Two bedrooms upstairs—one was Russell and Junior's, and the other one was Big Sis and my room. The one bedroom downstairs was Daddy and Thea-Thea's, with a small hallway and the stairs that separated the big kitchen where Thea-Thea worked her magic. We had a long back porch where part of the rooms upstairs covered. A little ways from the house was the "throne room"—the toilet.

Across from our big front yard lived Mr. Ed and Ms. Viv. Their house was a one-story house with three rooms, a front porch the length of the house, and an outside toilet.

My friend Pearlie lived in the last house on the right side with a fence that separated the yard from the Crow Pole. Between the Crow Pole and the last house was a piece of empty land where the men gathered to gamble and shoot dice, drink and have fun. Two big barrels sat off to the side of the Crow Pole, where the men warmed themselves when fall of the year rolled around.

The last house that stood by itself was where my friend Olive lived with her grandparents, the Leonards. It was a nice one-story house of four rooms and a front porch, which was kept pristine—as was their outside toilet. This little bungalow sat just below the foot of the steep hill leading up to the mines. The creek was the only thing separating the road to the foot of the hill. A car bridge was built for the vehicles.

Chapter Thirteen

Love Has No Color

Jerry and Junior had become buddies during the years my Thea-Thea worked for the family as their cleaning lady, babysitter, cook, you name it, until I came along and she said Daddy told her she didn't need to make it too hard on herself with two little ones.

I think Jerry was my first heartthrob. He always brought me candy or something when he came.

Thea-Thea would take Junior to work with her when he was little, and he and Jerry would play together while she worked. Jerry's mother was a schoolteacher.

The boys had remained friends all through the years, even though they were from two different worlds. They didn't see the difference in their color.

As they grew older, even after Thea-Thea had stopped working outside the home, Jerry's mom would drive him up to the foot of the hill and drop him off so he could play with Junior, but Junior never went to Jerry's house to play. It was never mentioned why.

One day, Jerry came to the house very upset. He said that they were moving to another state. His father had been transferred. He was heartbroken. He and Junior played their last day of cowboys and Indians in the backyard and around the house, as they were not allowed to go off the hill to play—stern orders from Jerry's mother.

As the evening passed and just before Jerry's father came to pick him up, they made a pact, a blood oath. They each very lightly nicked one of their wrists—one on the right, the other on the left—and mixed their blood. "Blood brothers forever," they both vowed.

Junior brooded over Jerry's leaving and got all of the attention. He was loving it.

Chapter Fourteen

HOW OLIVE CAME TO BE

The Leonards . . . well, what can I say—they are an odd couple, deeply religious but strange, and Ms. Leonard is a *hypocrite* . . . whatever that means.

I just happened to overhear Aunt Cellie telling the other women that she was a hypocrite.

Daddy would say, "Now dat's a strange pair if I ever seen one. Nice people, just a little strange."

"Yep, they strange all right, but Mable is mo' than strange. She got some *secrets* dat might git her in trouble one of these days," said Thea-Thea.

"Sho' ya right, HoneyBabe. I just hope Tee don't ever catch 'em. I hate to thank what might happen," Daddy said.

Mr. Leonard had a crook in his neck. I don't see how he walked, 'cause his head was almost on his shoulder. My Daddy said that he had been injured in the mines. It didn't seem to bother him; he just looked odd to me.

I would find myself looking at him when he was talking and not really hearing him 'cause my mind was on his neck. He would have to snap me back into reality by saying, "ClarrrrraBy, Olive is in her bedroom . . . . Did ya hear me, child?"

Daddy said, "Tee can sho' handle dat man-trip wit his neck like dat, 'cause he gotta lean to da side all da time anyhow."

"Oh, oh, yes sir, yes sir, Mr. Leonard, thank you." I was so embarrassed. I know he knew where my mind was, but he just shook his head as much as he could and walked back into the other room telling Ms. Leonard, "I thank dat child of Cal's is gonna be a little on da slow side or maybe she got a hearing problem, I don't know."

Ms. Leonard would reply, "Ya could be right, Tee. I thought da same thang, she always seems to be in another world when she comes over here, looking round and such, like she scared or somethin', ya know what I mean?"

"Yeah, I done noticed dat," replied Mr. Leonard.

Well, I've got news for them: anybody in their right mind would be scared if they saw all the stuffed animal heads they had hanging on every wall in the house. Deer heads everywhere; a big, black bear head just as you came in the door was staring you in the face. They even had a stuffed cat that they said was their pet. And it was always so dark in there! And a big, black car that looked like an ambulance. Geeeeee already, what ya expect? I might be a kid, but I'm smart you know.

I didn't make it a habit of visiting Olive, but when I did, she was glad to have me, 'cause she was one lonely child. Her room was like a sanctuary and immaculate, everything had its place. You didn't know whether to sit down or kneel. Her Bible sat on her nightstand and stayed on the same pages: Deuteronomy chapter 5.

She was one of my favorite playmates. I liked playing with her. We'd play on her floor with her doll and my favorite doll, which I would always bring with me. We would pretend to *be* the dolls and talk back and forth making up stories as we went along. She only had one doll, as they didn't believe in "lavish living," she said.

Well, I can't tell, what with all them dead heads on the wall, I thought. *Sommmmmebody's done some lavish killing or something in their day. I wonder who? Duh, Mr. Tightwad.*

They went to church down the road. "It's a *Holy Ghost* church, and Granddaddy gon' be a preacher!" Olive told me excitedly. "You gota go with me sometime, ClaraBy."

"Sure, why not," I said.

She and Ms. Mable dressed differently from the other women in the community—not that any of them had so much, but Ms. Mable made all of their clothes and they all looked the same, just different colors. The skirts and dresses were long with long sleeves. Olive was always neat and clean, though.

She was not their daughter, but the daughter of their only child, who (I found out by my Sherlock Holmes eavesdropping) had gotten in with the wrong crowd when she left home and had turned into a drunk and a prosti-something or other. So the Leonards had gone to Ohio and gotten Olive and brought her back to live with them.

All the ladies said that it was a good thing. Ms. Noon said, "Dat po' little thang was barely livin' when she got here. She was so po', ya could see her rib cage. Lawd knows they's too old to raise dat child, but whose gonna do it? They's doing da best they can . . . but they's a little strange though. Mable don't hardly say much, and ya can't visit her, 'cause ya don't know how to take her. I just know Tee gonna catch her one of these days, mark my word, mark my word."

Ms. Nellie said, "Dat child ain't got a clue what's happening in dat house while she got to sat on da porch for hours."

I often wondered why Olive would be sitting on the porch by herself some days. She would just play by herself, as she wasn't allowed off the porch during the week.

Chapter Fifteen

No Love Like Mother Love

"She better off here though," said Ms. Noon. "I tell ya," she said, "we don't know what dem chilluns of ours doing in these big cities. They's come in on holidays like they's living like kings and queens, but don't go visitin' 'em, honey-child, why ya thank ya in prison by da time they git through locking da door. CLING-CLANG-CHING-CHANG. Child, I knows what I's talking bout, I done seen fo' myself how my boy livin' . . . wit his lyin' ass. I thought he looked a little puny when he come home fo' Christmas, but we was so glad to see him, we didn't thank much 'bout it. He said he worked all da time."

"He was sharp as a tack, well y'all seed him, a lyin' scoundrel, come down here in dat big car and don't nobody pay no 'tention to da license plate where it's from, ya just glad yo child doin' good. Well, lo and behold, da license plate had Ill'noise license and he live in Detroit! I thought dat was strange, but I don't say nothing. Ain't dat a blip?" she said. "He done rented da car and was livin in a one-room apartment on da fifteenth flo' of a high-rise dat scared da bee-jee-bees outa me an Slim. Da elevata' lights was out; it smelt like pee; da people dat got on wit us scared us so bad, dat we got off on da fifth flo' and waited on another elevata." They's looked like they was hungry—ya hear me?—and we was da meal.

"Hee, heee, I can laugh now, but it weren't funny then. When we got to him after we got da call dat he was sick, we was shocked.

He had *pneumonee*, and was almost gone if we hadn't got him to da hos-pilal in time."

"He was playing guitar in a band, making good money, but spending it on women and booze, no insho-rance, *so he was playing doctor wit his life!*"

"We asked 'em why don't he come back home. He says he don' wanna work in no mines. Noooo, he wanted da bright lights of da city, an' it almost kilted him! He doing better now after dat near-death thang, but he still dranks like a fish and smokes like a train, woman after woman. I never seen da beat at da women dat came and went just in da little time we was there.

"They babied his ever' need, crying and carrying on. Two of 'em met up at da same time, a white'un an' a black'un . . . child, it was ON. They had to *escoat* 'em out da place, hee hee heee."

She continued, "Ya know, my daddy played da guitar and sang in a juke joint. My mama would always say, 'Ya can put a suit on a gorilla and a guitar in his hands and he can git all da *nookie* he want.' I tell ya, can't nobody say nothin' bout nobody's chilluns."

"Sho' ya right," said Ms. Noon. "All we can do is pray dat they 'member they raisin'."

"Amen," said Thea-Thea softly. "Amen."

God, I thought, *a gorilla in a suit, playing a guitar* . . . . I tried hard to think what size suit he would wear . . . And what in the world is *nookie*?

Olive had very *strick* rules that she had to follow. She could only come out to play on Friday evening and Saturday afternoon, and just like me, she had to be home way before dark. So most of the time, we were running up the road together, racing each other. She always got home before I did, but I beat her to the foot of my hill. We would holler from our porches. I'd say, "See you tomorrow!" and she'd reply, "LORD WILLING!"

I'd recall that my Thea-Thea would always end sentences like that when she was planning anything. "LAWD WILLING."

Chapter Sixteen

TIME WITH MY LUDIE

There was a large slate dump that burned and smoldered all the time above the road that was behind the row of houses where Ludie lived. It was on top of the hill and didn't seem to be a threat. Ludie took me walking up there almost every evening when it wasn't too cold or too hot. While we were walking, Ludie would tell me about heaven on that dirt road. Her stories were so mesmerizing.

She would say, "ClaraBy, there are angels all around us even though we can't see them, and one day, I am going to be one of the angels watching over you."

I said, "Ludie, how can you be an angel? I can see you."

She would say, "You'll understand it better as you get older. ClaraBy," she said, "I'm going to where I'll have a new body. I'm gonna run and play and jump rope, and everything!" she would squeal.

I said, "Oh, Ludie, can I go? Please, can I go with you? I'll show you how to jump hot pepper, double-dutch, and, and . . ."

"No, no, ClaraBy . . ." As we stopped walking, taking my hands in hers, she said, "You have to stay here and live on, and I'll see you when you get there. But right now, let's just enjoy each other. Okay?"

"Okay," I said, as we started to walk again, but I didn't quite understand why she wouldn't take me with her to this wonderful place. She even said she would be *flying*, "Gosh, I want to fly Ludie," I said.

"You will someday, ClaraBy, but it's not your time yet."

"But, Ludie, I don't know what you mean."

She said, "I know, but you will later . . . when you get older. You will. Remember the scripture I read to you where Jesus said for you not to be troubled or afraid and how He has already gone there to get our mansion ready?"

"Uh-huh," I said.

"Well, ClaraBy, He's *really* working on mine, and it's almost complete, and it's beautiful . . . with streets of gold, gates of pearl . . ." and on and on she went.

Excited, I said, interrupting her as I had had an enlightening thought. *"LUDIE, WHEN I GET THERE, WILL I HAVE TO EMPTY THE SLOP JAR?*

Ludie burst out laughing, "Oh, ClaraBy, baby, you are the only thing on this great earth that can make me laugh till I hurt." She was bent over with laughter. I started laughing with her.

"Whee," she said catching her breath, you'll understand it better as you grow, now run along, I'll be on the porch. Go hide-n-seek where I told you to hide."

We turned around 'cause Ludie couldn't walk very far. So off I went, flying with my little legs going as fast as they would go. Looking back at Ludie, who was taking her time walking, and waving at me and still laughing, I thought to myself, *Is this how it's gonna be when she goes away? She'll just drift out of my sight as I run ahead in life?*

Chapter Seventeen

Good Old Ms. Maxwell

There was a railroad track that ended where the black community began, and these huge, empty coal cars would be there. That was our Halloween scare, as they loomed in the dark and all kinds of weird sounds seemed to come from behind them, from the mountains. None of the little kids would walk that stretch of road alone.

The creek was the only calming thing along this stretch of road. We didn't know where it started, but it ran all the way past the last hollow. We had so much fun in the creek catching bullfrogs and swimming. The community had made a swimming hole by damming up the creek in the deepest part, which was located in front of Ms. Mae Maxwell's shanty.

"What y'all doing down dar?" she'd holler.

Aunt Cellie, who always took time with us younguns, would holler back, "Me, Ruth, and the kids making a swimming hole, Mae!"

Ms. Maxwell had saved everything she had ever gotten. Her three rooms were full of I don't know what—boxes and bags everywhere. Lord only knows what else was living with her. "Y'all younguns come git some goodies! I's got lots of 'em."

"Yes, ma'am," we'd holler back, knowing nobody ate Ms. Maxwell's cooking but her. But, being polite as we were taught, we'd go get what she had to offer, which was usually old cake. We'd pretend we were eating it, and throw it away as soon as we were out of her sight. Heee heee . . .

The house smelled to high heaven. A beautiful cat sat perched on the windowsill, almost looking unreal, but everyone knew that it was real. Ms. Maxwell loved that cat like it was her child. Ms. Maxwell would be seen getting it down the road once a month to the store, and getting it back up the hollow, refusing a ride if offered, winter or summer. Nobody really knew how old she was; they just said she was *old*. Some would say, "Oh, she's at least a hundred or so." Others would say, "Noooo, she ain't that old; she may be around eighty or so."

"Well, she in better shape than me, and I ain't nowhere near her age," Aunt Cellie said, laughing lightly.

After the swimming hole got finished, everybody was excited. We went swimming every chance we could. But we were not allowed to go swimming without an adult around, and we little ones were only allowed in the very shallow water.

I remember getting in the shallow water and slipping on a slimy rock. Drowning I was, I tell you! I was fighting underwater. I only remember Ms. Ruth pulling me up by my hair and laying me on the bank. I was almost gone, I tell you! I never went in again. That was when I really knew there was a God, 'cause I saw white lights down there. "Was I . . . was I near that place Ludie talked about?" Well, from then on, I would stand on the banks and watch the other kids splash and play in the water. No matter how much Aunt Cellie begged, I would not go back in.

One beautiful Saturday afternoon, the big boys were being *hip*, trying to impress the girls they had told about the swimming hole. The pool side was full of young boys and girls who had come up the hollow from the other camps down the road. The guys decided to compete with each other over who could hold their breath the longest underwater. Those who wanted to participate jumped in. One by one, they would come up. Then finally, Junior came up, and lo and behold, a snake was lying on the back of his neck! Everybody freaked, screaming and hollering. Junior went back down in the water and swam to shore, scared to death!

"What kind was it?" hollers Ms. Mae?

Aunt Cellie hollers back, "I don't care what kind it was, cause to me it may as well be a "boa constrictor, a python, or whatever other great snake you can name. a snake, is a snake is a snake, 'specially laying cross your neck."

Ms. Maxwell stood on her porch and screamed, *"STOP AN GIVE GOD DA GLORY!"* Everybody stopped screaming and fell on their knees and thanked God that Junior had not been bitten. Needless to say, that was the last of the swimming hole. They emptied it by tearing down the dam. They believe it was a water moccasin, never to be seen again.

CHURCH
TALKING BOUT A GOOD TIME

Ms. Maxwell was a deeply religious woman. She was the custodian of our little church, which she kept spotless.

Our little church was located on the hill above Ms. Maxwell's shanty. She would be the first one there every Sunday, rain or shine, ringing the bell. She wore black all of the time. They said she had worn it every since Mr. Maxwell died. She made all of her clothes, and was a very sweet lady . . . just couldn't cook.

In the winter time, Ms. Maxwell would have made the fire and got the building as warm as possible early that morning before she went back home to dress. The bell would toll every Sunday morning at 9:30 a.m. promptly. When we'd start gathering in the church, she would strike out with a song: *"I love da Lawd; He heard my cry an pitied ever' groan . . . ."*

By then, the church was beginning to fill up and the people coming through the door and anyone already there would join in and repeat the words in a beautiful melody. She would sing, *"Long as I live an trouble rise, I'll hasten to His throne."*

OOOOhhhh, my heart would be racing as Russell, Junior, and I ran over the hill, up the steps, and headed for the door. It was the highlight of my week. The church was always full on Sunday mornings for Sunday school as well as for church that followed.

You could hear the singing in the summertime from a great distance 'cause all of the windows were up. Everybody seemed to know that it was going be a shouting good time today, and this was just Sunday school!

There were three classes taught straight from the Bible. The *little* kids, which was my class; the middle-age kids, which was Russell and Junior's class; and the adult class. Our teacher would ask simple questions, such as "Who was da baby Jesus's mother?" and "Who was found in a basket by Pharoah's daughter?"

It was exciting to know the answers, 'cause Ms. King could mix the questions up and kind of make you have to figure it out. We knew she had to work all week getting that lesson together. She seemed to enjoy stumping the class. She should've been a school teacher. She would say, "Class, Moses went upon da mountain to receive da Ten Commandments, but, who brought them down from da mountain?"

Well, the answer was simple, but the way she asked it was a little complicated and made you think. So we stuttered and stumbled around until finally, Olive said, "Moses brought them down." She looked at us as if to say "Duh." (Olive was allowed to come to my church for Sunday school only. Afterwards, she ran home to go to her church.)

Ms. King said, "Very good, Olive; dat's right." Some of us were scratching our head.

Poor J. J. was still thinking when Sunday school was over. He went up to Ms. King and said, "Ms. King, how could Moses bring them down if he was up on the mountain?"

"Well," she laughed lightly and patted him on the head and explained it to him until he understood it. I heard her say as I was passing, "J. J., you have to thank now," as she explained it.

He finally said, "Oooohh, I git it now."

Chapter Eighteen

WEIRDO!

Old man G-Baby lived in the shanty that was at the foot of the hill below the *(ooooooo, eeeeeeeek)* cemetery, which was a plot of land the coal company had given to the black community to bury their dead. It was a quiet place around the hill from Mr. G-Baby's shanty, with a dirt road that led up to the steps cut out of the dirt, leading up to the burial sites. It sat upon a hill surrounded by trees, and no grass grew over the graves because the trees were so tall they completely blocked out the sun. It was as if God Himself was the caretaker. Every grave marker was still visible, and even though they were tin, and some very old, you could still read some of the names and years on them. It really wasn't a scary place once you were up there; it was almost serene, cool and shady all the time.

All of us kids were scared of Mr. G-Baby though. He would come to the door and squall loudly as he beat on his chest like a wild man. He had a long, white beard and a head full of white bushy hair, and he stunk, jeez, did he stink. He never, ever bathed or shaved. We would take off running and screaming. If you told on him, the grownups would just say, "Ah, he just playing wit y'all. He knows ya scared," as they laughed at our silliness.

On Halloween, all of the community kids would go up the hollow to each community for candy and other goodies. We were not allowed down the road.

Anyone who had three—or four-year-old brothers and sisters were responsible for them, so we would band together to care for them, holding their hands, swinging them while they squealed with laughter.

We passed by Mr. G-Baby's house, which was never visited, at any time. Even the teenagers would not go there.

On our way back down the hollow, we were taking our time eating some of the goodies and laughing and talking just at the crack of dusk. Lo and behold, from up on the cemetery hill came this monster running and howling! Everybody took off running, leaving the very little ones all to themselves as we ran for our lives. I mean, I was hauling butt, leaving some of the older ones in the dust. When we got to Ms. Maxwell's shanty, we stopped and looked back. The little children were scared to death standing in the middle of the road screaming and crying. Well, the older kids knew they had to get them. They hollered to them to run as they ran toward them. The little ones were too scared to run, so the bigger kids had to go all the way to the front of Mr. G-Baby's shanty. He came out of his house laughing up a storm. We were so mad when we figured out the monster was him all the time.

He said, "I got ya, didn't I?"

He had made a cape out of a black tarp that when he ran with his arms spread out looked like a I-don't-know-what, maybe a giant black bat.

Well, he had killed the spirit of Halloween for all of us from that time on.

THANK YOU, MR. G-BABY!

I DON'T THINK ANY OF US NEEDED THE USUAL DOSE OF "CASTOR OIL" WE HAD TO TAKE AFTER EATING ALL OF THE GOODIES, AS HE HAD SCARED THE S—WELL, YOU GET THE PICTURE.

After that, the next Halloweens were spent in our camp with a fire to roast wieners and marshmallows. Aunt Cellie would have someone make the fire in the big barrel drums out by the Crow Pole. She would tell everyone to bring a clothes hanger, which was bent to make a long stick to hold onto, so we could roast our marshmallows and wieners, and your own drinking jar for the homemade lemonade.

The adults would bring goodies and their children down the hollow. A table was set in front of the Crow Pole with all of the goodies on it. We had a lot more fun with music and dancing and eating. Even the adults would join in. It turned into an annual thing that was joined by other parents and kids from other camps. It was almost always on a school night, so it was done pretty early and over by nine o'clock. But when it was on a Saturday, man, it was fun for *everybody*. People would have two or three barrels burning for roasting wieners and marshmallows, and the adults would have an outdoor-dancing-good-time, and we got to join in.

Chapter Nineteen

COMBING THROUGH THE FOREST

Mr. Man got his looks from his mother mostly, complexion and all, just not as high yellow, medium maybe. I don't know who he got his hair from though, 'cause it was kinky and bushy.

Poor Paula didn't inherit any of her ancestral hair from either side of the family, but she had plenty of it that hung way past her little shoulders. Her head was something to tackle, which seemed to be my task.

Big Sis said, "ClaraBy, you braid so well, why don't you do Paula's hair for me?"

"Sure," I said joyfully. Paula was my little Boo, but I didn't know what I was getting myself into. I had been braiding and plaiting hair since I could remember on my white dolls who all had long, blonde hair. I was just like my Aunt Idella—I loved to do me some hair.

So I got my comb and grease and went to Big Sis's to fix up my little Boo, whose hair had been freshly washed. I sat behind her and began to try to comb through the forest. She had a head full of medium brown hair, and it was standing all over her head like a bush. Needless to say, the fight was on. She screamed and wallowed, crying as if I were killing her.

Big Sis never said a word. She would pass through the room going to the kitchen as if we weren't even there. I was so frustrated I didn't know what to do.

I'd bribe Paula with candy and promises, and she would sit back down, only until I tried to drag the comb through her hair again, and then the fight resumed. I finally ended up giving her two puffs, one on each side.

I know now why Big Sis would say, "I can't do nothing with this girl's hair; it's a never-ending battle."

Thea-Thea would say, "Oh, she just tender-headed, dat's all."

Well, call it what you want, she wasn't having no part of getting braids. Only when she had gotten so tired and fallen asleep was I able to ease the comb through her hair with tender care so as not to wake her. I ended up having succeeded in putting four big long plaits on her little head.

"Whee, I'm glad that's over, and you can have your job back," I told Big Sis.

She laughed and said, "Thanks for trying."

"You welcome!" I replied, running home. "Never again, and I mean "*NEVER AGAIN!*"

The next camp above Mr. Man's parents was the other, *white* camp. Sometimes when I would visit Janice, the white kids would play with us. We'd play hop-scotch and rock school on the steps. The boys would play marbles. Beth was the little girl who really won my heart. She was a tiny thing at three, and she would run and jump in every mud puddle she could find, barefooted. Her mother would scold her, clean her up, and send her back out; well, she'd end up in the same way every time, mud puddle to mud puddle. We'd laugh our heads off at her. She knew she was the star.

Chapter Twenty

The Wooden Throne

Our outside toilet was as clean as the house itself, 'cause Russell and Junior had to scrub the porches and toilet *every* Saturday with *lye water*. Heeeee, heeeeee . . .

They would be mumbling and grumbling and scrubbing.

Thea-Thea was a drill sergeant when it came to cleanliness.

It seemed as if I was always the first one to have to do the honors after it was clean and dry . . . Heeee, heeee . . . I loved doing that. Junior would scream, "Thea-Thea, ClaraBy is tracking in dirt, and we just cleaned it!"

"Buuuuuuut, Thea-Thea, I gotta goooooooo . . . real . . . bad!" I was a little menace and knew it. Junior would call me a little spoiled brat, as I stuck my tongue out at him going into the great "wooden throne" door which stood a little ways from the house.

The *Sears* catalog was our friend. I would look at the pictures as I sat over the round hole that was the seat and pick out the clothes and things I was going to buy when I got the money. After I did my business, I'd tear the page out and wipe my little bottom. Rough, rough, rough, but who knew? There was nothing else. It was a luxury we could afford, big and thick and it lasted a looooong time.

But then, there was *the little white* throne called a slop jar, our inside toilet. It was kept clean as a whistle too, and I learned very early that it was my job to empty it and keep it clean daily . . . *eeeegag!* It was emptied every morning, and brought in the house before dark from the outhouse . . . Russell and Junior had to make sure that the old mop and a bucket of water was sitting close by, so if necessary, I could... well, you get the idea... *uugggghh*... The only good thing about that chore was that I would spend time with Little Red who was growing like a weed.

"HERE THEY COME!" hollered Junior. The honey dippers were coming to clean out the *toilets*. Everybody in the community had been waiting for them, as the holes were getting *pret-ty* full. I had asked Daddy a million, zillion questions about the ... *stuff*. Well... *stuff* wasn't exactly the word I wanted to use, but I knew it was the one I had better use.

"Baby Girl," he said, "ya gonna see a change."

Not exactly what I wanted to hear. I wanted to know where they were going to take ... the stuff How did they get it out of the hole? Could they find my teddy bear that I had dropped down in there?

Daddy also said that they sometimes covered the old hole over with heavy rocks and plenty of dirt and patted it down. Then they would dig another hole and set the throne over it.

"Okay already!" This was my very first time, and I was curious ... and very nosy. No wonder our garden was so beautiful and full every year!

Chapter Twenty-One

LIVING FOR THE WEEKEND

Friday, miner's payday, and parrr-ty time! Daddy would go to the company store, upstairs to where the payroll office was and get his payday. Some men wouldn't have a payday to pick up, because they had spent all of it in the company store, and so they had nothing. But nobody went hungry, and everybody pulled together, borrowing a cup of sugar or flour across the fences, just whatever to make a meal.

We were a happy community and the grownups seemed to have a lot of fun. They prepared for the weekend, holding conversations across the road and over the banisters to their neighbors.

"Yea, child!" Ms. Nellie would holler, "I'm coming as soon as Slim gets home."

The Friday weekend party started when the *man-trip* emerged out of the tunnel and the women knew their men were coming home. The man-trip was the coal car that carried the men in and out of the mines. That's what my daddy told me.

The men coming down the hill seemed to be happier on paydays, laughing and talking, eager to get the weekend started.

The children ran to meet their daddies; the wives started up the record players. The fresh fish truck had run, and fresh fish was frying in every house, smelling um, um good. Old man Bob had made his weekly delivery of homemade moonshine, so the party was on. My little community was a partying, card-playing, church-going, good-time place.

The card players would go from house to house, depending on whose house was having the game and play *pitty-pat*. Thea-Thea and Daddy loved to play cards. Sometimes, some of the gambling men wouldn't even change out of their bankers the whole weekend. They would go home, eat and hurry to the house where the game was going to be so as to be one of the first to play. Sometimes the games went on all weekend long.

The men, one at a time, would take turns snatching a nap in their bankers behind the stove. The women would lie across the bed. The house lady would sell sandwiches and drinks. The women who had kids went home only to cook and feed them and were right back at it. This went on sometimes until late Sunday night for the men.

The women seemed to give up on Sunday morning, 'cause Sunday was worship day, and they all went to church. Some of the men, who went to church, would leave the game in time to get home and change clothes, and right back at it after church was out. The rest of the men, including my daddy, would just go to work as they had left on Friday, if the games lasted that long.

The women would drift off one by one, either when they got broke or when they would have had enough knowing they had to get the kids up for Sunday school. The men never seemed to give up; even if they had gone broke, they hung around hoping their cut-buddy would throw them something....

"Git it, girl!" Somebody would holler when Ms. Nibby started to dance. She had a behind on her as big and round as a #3 tub, and she could roll it like nobody could. She was famous for *riding the mule*. Man, the floor would clear when the music got her riding the mule; she would reach down and pat the floor with the palms of her hands and roll that big tub around and round and up and down. The man who thought he could dance would try to keep up with her. He would be humping and bumping and sweating.

We would be upstairs in my room looking down through the vent, as my room was right over Thea-Thea and Daddy's bedroom where all the dancing took place. Junior and Russell would move me out of the way and take up the whole little vent.

Well, I'd just do my own thing by imitating Ms. Nibby riding the mule, she had nothing on me.

"Sit your fast tail down," Russell would say, soft and harsh. "I'm gonna tell Thea-Thea on you," as they would go back to looking and giggling softly, with their hands over their mouths. When they couldn't hold it any longer, they would get up and fall on the bed, rolling with laughter softly, so as not to be heard. Then it was *my* chance to take over the hole and get my eyes full.

By now, *"CALDONIA, CALDONIA, what makes your big head so hard"* had ended and everybody was swaying to a slow song: *"oooh, ooooh, baby, you done lost yo good thang now."*

"Honey Child!" Ms. Nibby would squall as she wiped the sweat from her brow with her apron. They really seemed to be having big fun. It seemed that if you were the one that hadn't gotten into the card game, then you partied until some poor soul went broke and had to get up and give up their seat. The game played seven players.

Somebody would holler out, *"Next!"* and in the next sucker would run, and the poor sucker who was broke would then join in the fun, trying to drown out his or her sorrow of losing maybe all they had until the next time.

Daddy couldn't read or write, but he could count like nobody's business, and nobody, and I do mean nobody dared to cheat him. If you borrowed something from him, it was etched in stone in his mind, to the penny, and he didn't take no mess about it.

I heard him tell Mr. Slim, "Now, Slim, dat makes three dollars. I want my money come payday."

"Okay, Cal, okay, man," Mr. Slim would say, glad to have the money to stay in the game a little bit longer.

We would finally get tired of watching the show and go to bed, because we knew we had to get up early if it was Saturday and do our chores. But if it was Sunday, there was a known rule in the house: Sunday school and church. I would take my bath and get it over with, which was in a new, long, tin tub. I could almost lie down in it.

"ClaraBy, hurry up," Russell would holler.

"Yeah," Junior would chime in, "hurry up, *shoot.*"

"Thea-Thea, ClaraBy won't git out the tub!" he'd snitch.

"ClaraBy!" she'd say forcefully, "hurry up, girl; da boys gotta git their baths too."

Well ... out I'd come, passing by them and looking at them with that little-sister disdain. With my towel wrapped around me up to my neck, I'd give them a long tongue licking, squinting up my nose, ummmmmmmmmmmmmmmm!

But this day was my first time in the BIG NEW TUB, and I was really miffed, so instead of sticking out my tongue, I did the unthinkable: I put my thumb in my nose and gave them the finger wave just as Thea-Thea was coming up behind them.

Well, I can only tell you, that with my little body still being wet, that I looonnnged for that place Ludie had told me about. "PLEASE TAKE ME AWAY QUICKLY, SHE'S KILLING ME!" I tell you, I have never, ever put my thumb in my nose and waved from that day forward. Thank you, merciful GOD, for allowing her to stop at the point of what I thought was surely my demise.

My two big-headed brothers were savoring the moment, although they pretended not to when they came upstairs. I was still sniffling and snorting. I heard them snickering—I've got good ears. *They'll pay,* I promised myself, *they'll pay.*

So that night before the party started, I locked my door so that they couldn't get in, and they wouldn't dare be seen trying to make me open the door as anyone passing in the hallway would see them. Every once in a while I would hear a soft knock and them whispering, "ClaraBy, Baby Girl, ClaraBy, Baby Girl." *Heee heeeee, heeeeeeee ...*

"ClaraBy, Baby Girl," I mimicked. "Pay back, my brothers, pay back!"

Chapter Twenty-Two

YIPPEE!

"ClaraBy, ClaraBy, wake up, time to go to school," said Thea-Thea.

"OH MY!" *It's my first day of school, I'm so excited! I've been waiting for this day all of my life,* I think. Thea-Thea had bought me a brand new dress, new black-and-white shoes, and a brand new pair of socks for my first day.

She was so excited, crying and saying, "My baby is going to school. I can't believe ya going to school! You done growed up so fast on me. My baby . . ." she said, as she squeezed me.

She plaited my hair in three long plaits—one big part on the side, one to the left, and one to the right, with a part down the middle in the back—and put hair ribbons on each one. She gave me a pep talk as we were going out the door and all the way down the steps. "Russell, Junior, take care of yo sister, ya hear?"

"Yes, ma'am," they replied.

Every mother in the community was standing on their porches to see their children off to school. Even Ludie was on the porch this early morning the first day of school.

She said, "You look so pretty, ClaraBy."

"Thank you, Ludie," I replied, waving to her as I passed her house. I felt so special, like a big girl.

My Big Sis was standing on the porch to see me on my special day. "You look so pretty, ClaraBy," she said. "Now, remember what I told you about listening to your teacher," she said.

"Okay, Big Sis," I replied. She was so big now that she didn't feel like doing anything. I felt so sorry for her. Ooooh well, this was *my* special day . . . .

We had to walk down out of the hollow to get to our one-room school, which was grades one through four. The little school only had little, old used desks, a pot-bellied stove for heat, and a blackboard; it had a big old desk in the front of the little desks for the teacher to sit at and a cabinet for the books.

The first-comers had to learn from the older ones to place our lunch bag on the windowsill.

Thea-Thea had gotten my school supplies from the company store: paper, pencils, glue, and a pair of little scissors.

Ms. Deskins, our teacher, taught all of the grades, which were divided up in four rows, one desk behind the other. She lived down the road apiece and rode the big yellow bus up the road to the school.

The big kids went about five miles down the road to another school, which was the grade school and the middle school, and the other bigger kids rode the same bus another ten miles to go to the big high school. They got to ride the *big* yellow bus that was parked at the company store waiting for them.

After my brothers walked me to school that first day, Russell said, "Baby Girl, you be good now, okay?"

"Okay," I said. They turned and ran to get on the school bus, driven by this nice man called Mr. Luster, a black man. I was confused, because a white man driving a big yellow bus would come up in the hollow every morning all the way up to the end of the hollow to pick up the white kids. I had seen this bus, it seemed, all my life coming and going up and down the hollow. I wondered why, but it was never discussed, so it didn't seem to bother us; we had a good time, winter time and spring, walking up and down the road, stopping at the tipple to get a fresh drink of water out of the outside spigot, playing tag and other games all the way home. We had snowball fights when it snowed.

I really liked school, Reading, Writing, and Arithmetic. We had to share books, which were raggedy hand-me-downs, but we loved reading about "Run, Jane, run" or whoever. Every time Ms. Deskins asked a question, my little hand was up waving and squirming in my seat, ready with the answer. *Man*, I thought, *I'm pretty smart.*

The company store and doctor's office were adjoined, so if any one of us got sick, we would have to go over to the office to see the company doctor.

Dr. Austin knew if we were really sick or if we were faking, so he had a hefty supply of sugar pills for the fakers. He would only give us one, but it was worth it—we found out later it was candy.

Russell had no problem going to school. He was in high school and loving it. But Junior, who went to the middle school, was a problem. He hated going to school. He would stand at the gate begging Thea-Thea to let him stay home.

"Please, Thea-Thea, I'll give you my quarter to play your numbers if you let me stay," he'd say.

I would walk by him and call him a "pussy," as I passed.

Tears falling he would scream, "Ahhhhhh, Thea-Thea, ClaraBy said a bad word!"

"No I didn't, Thea-Thea!"

"Git on down dat road, boy—and ya better go to school!" she would reply.

Junior fussed at me all the way down the hill, and I joined the younger ones who surrounded me. We ran on ahead of the bigger ones, squealing with delight.

The one thing that all the kids really hated about going to school was, *Blue Monday, how I hate blue Monday . . . have to work like a slave all day!"* Man was that a true song!

Every Monday, all the kids dreaded coming home from school. It was beginning to get cold, which made Mondays just that much more miserable. Junior and Russell had to wake up earlier on Monday mornings to make the fire under the tubs full of water that they had filled up the evening before. There was a special pit that Daddy had made to fix the fire in and sat the tubs on top of sort of like an outdoor grate. It was wash day, and we'd be eating pinto beans and corn bread, as that was the quick Monday meal; the beans cooked all day and didn't need that much attention. Clothes hung on everything. The clothes lines were full, the banisters, the fence, the backs of chairs, everywhere a piece of clothing could be hung was covered.

The house had a damp chill to it, because of all of the wet clothes. Some took longer to dry than others.

Now that I was a "big girl," I had to retrieve all the clothes off of everything but the clothes line, as I wasn't quite tall enough to reach that yet. Junior and Russell brought in the clothes off the numerous lines and piled them up on the bed. Some would be stiff from the cold and not yet quite dry. So then, they would take the place of the dry clothes over the backs of chairs and anything else.

The only thing that was satisfying about that day was my *pretty, starched can-cans* that were spread over the lines in beautiful colors. Three of them: sparkling white, baby blue, and pretty in pink. My mama would starch my petticoats so stiff that they made my dresses and skirts stand out like an umbrella so pretty. I felt like a princess! I also loved to chomp on a hunk of starch from the box.

Thea-Thea would proceed to sprinkle the clothes down with water, fold them in the shape of dough, and place them in baskets. She said that was to "season them to make them easier to iron." Sheets, pillow cases, dish towels in one basket; shirts and other pieces of clothing in other baskets. I had to match the socks, fold one into the other, and separate my bloomers, the boys *drawls* (underwear), Daddy's long john's, and Thea-Thea's bloomers—MAN, were they huge!

The clothes would be set aside to season for ironing the next day. Thank God, I didn't have to iron . . . yet!

Thea-Thea was a stay-at-home mom now, but she took in ironing from the affluent white women, so she had her work cut out for her when the husband of the woman she ironed for delivered the baskets of hard and dry clothes. They didn't even sprinkle 'em down. What a crock.

One of my worst whippings ever was one night, I let Junior, talk me into *doing the unthinkable*. Thea-Thea had company—Ms. Nellie, Aunt Cellie, Ms. Noon and Ms. Sadie were sitting in the kitchen laughing and talking. Junior thought it would be funny if I put on a pair of Thea-Thea's big, white bloomers and go downstairs acting like I was grown or something.

Well, Thea-Thea didn't think it was funny at all. She had me go pick my own poison off the tree. She was livid. "Ya thank ya grown? Well, I'll show ya!" she hollered behind me as I was walking slowly to the nearest tree.

I broke off the tiniest *switch I* could. Well, she sent me right back, saying, "Ya don't want *me* to git it, do ya?".

Needless to say, there was some hopping and screaming going on that time with me trying to explain . . . but she wasn't listening to a thing I had to say.

Junior was dying laughing when I finally whimpered myself back upstairs. I called him everything I could think of, but it only made it worse. He teased me all evening and then told everybody about my fate the next morning on our way down the road to school.

I was the laughing stock of the camp that morning. Junior had teamed up with the other *ugly* boys and was showing them how I was jumping and hollering. They were having a good old time at my expense.

Janice, one of my best friends, turned around swiftly, and said very slowly, *"JUNNN-IOR,* if you say one more word about ClaraBy, I'm gonna beat the *holy shit* outa ya."

The whole group stopped. They looked like they had been hypnotized. Then the boys all started in on Junior, laughing and teasing him about being beat up by a girl. I had the last laugh after all. *Wheeeee-heeee-heeeee.*

Junior came over to me and said, "Okay, Baby Girl, I'm sorry. I was just paying you back."

Down the road we all went, racing each other until we got to the white camp; then we slowed down and walked mannerly, speaking only if anyone was on their porch, "Good morning."

We were always taught to be polite, and there seemed to be an unspoken way of saying *be polite especially to* WHITE PEOPLE.

Chapter Twenty-Three

Summertime, Summertime

The year passed so fast. I was promoted to the second grade! Boy was I excited, running home with my report card to show my Thea-Thea and Daddy. Russell and Junior had passed too. All of us had passed, but Junior had made it by the skin of his chinny chin-chin. But he was still excited that he had passed.

Russell said excitedly, "Next year, I've got big plans—I'm going to join the band!" He wanted to play the *saxophone*.

Junior said, "Man, why you wanna be in the band when you can play football and be near them cheerleaders?"

Russell replied, "*Man*, are you crazy? Have you seen them majorettes? Now that's who *I* wanna be near. Have you seen how they whip their skirts and twirl them things in their hand? There's one in particular that I got my eye on—man, is she *fiiiine*."

Russell was showing him some of the moves the band players did, and that really got him going. He said they just know how to make the song more than what you hear by the way they move. "I'll have the girls swooning!" he laughed. "Just like Junior Walker!" And he started humming a tune with his hands as if he was blowing the sax.

Junior just said, "Whatever floats yo boat, man."

Daddy just smiled and shook his head as if to say "Dat's my boys."

Thea-Thea said, "Well, I know one thang: ya both had better keep yo eyes on them *grades*."

"Yes, ma'am," they said in unison as they ran upstairs playfully punching each other. I was just savoring the moment with my family . . . and the last day of school. HALLELUJAH!

"Whee! Summertime, summertime!" I was going to Virginia to stay with my first cousin Katherine all summer.

Every summer in the past, my Aunt Idella, Uncle Robert, Big Mama, and cousin Katherine would come to our house, but this time, we were going to their house. Oh boy, Oh boy!

Thea-Thea was going to take me on the big Trailways bus. She was going to stay for a week with Big Mama and Aunt Idella. It was a vacation for her, but also, it was to see how I could accept her leaving me on my own, as this would be my first time out of her sight.

It was so exciting getting on the big bus. We went all the way to the back and sat down. Thea-Thea had packed us a lunch in a shoe box. She had deviled eggs, homemade souse meat, homemade rolls, cake, and a milk bottle full of water. Umm, umm. It was like going on a picnic.

So, when the bus stopped at different stops, Thea-Thea said we would only get off if we had to pee, which we didn't have to—as Thea-Thea said, "If you don't have to go real bad, we can make it without getting off."

I didn't think about it at the time, but none of the black people got off the bus when we stopped. So I held it. It wasn't so bad, 'cause I went to sleep after eating my belly full.

It only took about three hours to get to the other station where Uncle Robert was waiting for us.

Everything was so big and beautiful in Virginia. I was amazed at the buildings and things. People were hustling and bustling around. I was a fascinated little girl.

Uncle Robert was standing there with his handsome self, grinning from ear to ear. "Y'all have a good trip?" he asked.

"Yes Lawd, *whee*," Thea-Thea said, "I'm sho' glad we made it."

"Come on," he said, "Let me git yo bags."

My head was spinning as I tried to take in all of the scenery. As we came around the curve, on the right, there was the biggest cemetery I had ever seen. Big statues of angels and monuments were everywhere.

Over in the valley, across the creek was a little community. We went down the hill and around the curve over the railroad tracks and turned left, through the white community which was so pristine and nice, down another little knoll and across the railroad tracks, again in a semi-circle as it was the same track we had crossed, and onto the dirt road of the Negro section where we pulled up in the yard, honking the horn. It was a family tradition to blow the car horn whenever you were nearing your destination, this made the entrance more exciting.

Big Mama, Aunt Idella, and Katherine were standing on the porch, waving and hollering when they saw the car. Big Mama was beside herself as she came off the porch, tears running down her cheeks. She grabbed Thea-Thea and rocked her with kisses. Then she saw me, and grabbed her own cheeks saying, "Thea-Thea, this ain't dat baby is it? Lawd, she done growed since last year!" as she grabbed me and showered me with kisses.

Aunt Idella was hysterical. *"Come on in da house!"* she shouted as she hugged and kissed us, grabbing Thea-Thea by the hand.

Katherine came up to me and said, "Hey, cousin, how you doing?"

"Fine," I said, "how you doing?"

"Fine," she said. "Come on, let me show you my room." We ran inside and up the steps.

"Wow," I said. Her room was so nice. She had a big, big bed, a radio and a pick-up (a record player); dolls were everywhere. We squealed with glee. She was so happy I had come to stay the summer. We were the same age and liked the same things.

"Mama, can ClaraBy and I go play?" Katherine asked my aunt Idella.

This would be my very first time away from home without my Thea-Thea, so I may as well test the water on how I'm gonna handle it when she leaves me. I knew to ask Thea-Thea if I could go play, so I said, "Thea-Thea may I go?"

Aunt Idella answered "Yes Kat, you know what to do, don't let me have to send for ya."

Thea-Thea said, "okay ClaraBy, ya may as well get yo feet wet, go on.

"Yes, ma'am we said, and off we went. We had lots of fun. There were so many kids to play with. I was the *new kid in town*, so I got the royal treatment. Believe you me, we were back home and upstairs in Katherine's room wayyyyyy before dark. You see, Aunt Idella don't play just like my Thea-Thea.

Aunt Idella was a beautician. Man, could she lay some marcel curls down; she could wave out of this world. She was a *pro* at what she did and stayed busy.

Big Mama was the hair washer, getting the ladies ready one by one as they came in, wrapping their heads up in a fresh clean towel, massaging their hair semi-dry, and then placing them under the hair dryer. She would then comb their hair out and grease it, plait it in four plaits—those who had any to plait.

Ms. Louise, who lived just up the road, and a regular customer, was a beautiful little thing. She had to be way up there in age. Her hair was snow white, until Big Mama did something to it that turned it into a beautiful silver blue, and after Aunt Idella pressed and curled it, well, it was the a *masterpiece* of beauty! It hung down way past her shoulders, straight with only a turned-under curl. Beautiful, I tell you, beautiful . . .

I thought my aunt and uncle were rich. They had a very nice house and had this shiny, huge car. They were *living,* child;, I mean living!

Uncle Robert was a coal miner too, and the only black man in the community who had a car, so he drove three other men in the community to work with him.

He was a faithful fisherman in his spare time, and he and his buddies had caught fresh fish for our arrival. It was *on* now. Aunt Idella, Big Mama, and Thea-Thea got to cooking it. They invited friends over for the evening, with fresh fish frying, music playing, dancing, and having a real good time.

Big Mama seemed oblivious to the noise in the other part of the house. She was in her favorite chair, which was a big barber chair in the beauty shop part of the house, crocheting and whistling to herself. She had a way of entertaining herself besides crocheting by placing her fingers between each hand and twirling her thumbs over and over forward and backward as she whistled to herself, stopping only to spit snuff in the coffee can she kept close. She seemed to enjoy that so much. Her mind seemed to be out-of-body. Soon, she would make her way upstairs to bed.

These houses were made completely different from ours. They had more rooms—five downstairs and three smaller ones upstairs. Their outside toilets were different too. They were located down a row of steps from the house, and were spotless. They had two to a family! I was amazed.

Big Mama's room was quite unique, to say the least. Being as she was part Indian, there were signs of her heritage that she had kept through the years. Odd feathers and other relics that had been passed down from her Indian and African heritage. They were neatly placed on her dresser. She had something hanging over her door as you entered, and she addressed it in some way whenever she came in or went out. Her presence commanded respect. There was just something about her that was . . . I guess you could say *divine*.

She would cradle us in her big lap and hum tunes never spoken, until we fell asleep. Climbing up in that big barber chair into her soft lap after a hard day at play was like being in a feather bed. She had the kind of arms I loved to roll between my fingers: big, flabby, and juicy just like I like 'em . . . . She spoiled me *rot'en*.

There was a special dried flower she kept in her old Bible. She told us that it had been placed in Grand Daddy's hand by her request from her flower garden, and before they closed the coffin, she had taken it out of his hand and kept it ever since. That was her way of holding hands with him one more time.

Quilts were everywhere. Some were finished, some weren't. She gave them as gifts for different occasions: weddings, birthdays, Christmas presents. She even had made all of her grandchildren little ones for their cribs. I still had mine at the foot of my bed.

She had several quilts that were from her mother, worn and faded but beautiful. She was a master quilter and could sew anything. She saved every piece of old clothing and turned them into works of art—just as she could make a meal out of practically nothing, as I learned later in years.

There was a picture of her and my grandpa hanging on the wall. I was amazed, as no one ever talked about him. He seemed to be looking right at me. I turned my head this way and that, trying to see who he favored, and realized in shock, that my brother Russell, who was named after him, looked so very much like him. No wonder the kid was Big Mama's favorite—and she made no bones about it. Now, I really understood why . . . .

* * *

The day that Thea-Thea was to leave for home, she was quite concerned that I was going to be homesick when she left. She sat me down on the immaculate couch that was covered with plastic in the living room, which was the most beautiful room I had ever seen. And with my little hands in hers, she said, "Baby Girl, I'm leaving today; ya gonna be all right?"

"Yes, ma'am," I said, "I'm having so much fun."

"Okay then, you mind yo Aunt Idella, Uncle Robert, and Big Mama ya hear?"

"Yes, ma'am," I replied, "I'm gonna be a good girl!" I said with glee.

So off we went to the bus station. Katherine and I danced around and around, hands in hand with glee in the parking lot. We were gonna have fun, fun, fun.

There was one family that was quite interesting at the end of the camp—the Spencers. Man, there was a brood of them. Their father was a retired army man who walked proudly . . . and undoubtedly carried a big stick. There were thirteen of them, ranging in all ages and in all colors—light, dark, medium brown, you name it. But they all looked alike, so when you saw one of them, you knew who they were.

When Mr. Spencer was officially released from the army, still a young man, Uncle Robert took him to get a job in the mines where he worked.

One evening, after Uncle Robert had come home from work, I suddenly realized that he was *clean* every day he came home. Now, how can this be? He worked in the mines like my daddy did, so why was he and the men who rode in his nice clean car, all clean too?

"Uncle Robert," I said, "how come you don't come home all dirty, with your face covered with dust, and . . . and where are your bankers?" I was puzzled and I wanted to know, so well, you know me, I was pretty nosy.

Uncle Robert and Aunt Idella were sitting on the front porch after the delicious supper we had enjoyed. Kat and I were playing jack rocks when I because curious as to why he never bathed at home.

"Well Bee-Bee (his pet nickname for me), Over here in Virginia we got different companies dat manage da mines. So when contract time come up, (dat's da 'greement between da company an us union brothers). Us union brothers demanded a bathhouse and we got it long wit a lota other thangs we needed. So when we git to work, we change into da bankers in da bathhouse, and when work day is over, I look just like Calvin covered with black dust. Only difference is, I can bathe 'fore I come home. I brangs my bankers home in da old bag in da trunk of da car, two times a month for washing."

"Oh, I wish my daddy had a bathhouse."

Well, Ms. Lessie Spencer was visited by the big bird again that summer. I wondered, *How did that bird get way over here in Virginia?* But I didn't ask no questions. No sirreeeee! This made fourteen—you hear me?—*fourteen!*

It seemed as if time passed so fast. I had played all I wanted to, but now I was ready to go home. I was homesick. I missed my daddy and Thea-Thea.

So one Saturday morning, Uncle Robert, Aunt Idella, Big Mama, and Katherine took me home. Around and around and up and down the mountains we went.

When we left the highway and started up the hollow to my house, Uncle Robert started blowing his horn. He toot-tooted it a couple of times as we passed the company store, again as we went through the white camp, waving at people on the porches.

But then, as we passed the white camp and started up the road past the last house, he bore down on the horn in a constant toot, *tooooooooooooooooooooooooot!*

I got so excited I could hardly stand it. Everybody knew that we were coming, so excitement was high in the little camp. It was two weeks before school was to start, and my aunt Idella had bought me some new clothes. I was in heaven and could hardly wait for school to start!

As the car pulled up to the foot of the hill, Thea-Thea was jumping up and down on the porch screaming, "My baby, my baby!"

Daddy was at the Crow Pole, which was full of men laughing and talking, getting really excited knowing Uncle Robert was coming and the party was gonna be *on*.

My daddy came across the road to open the door, helping Big Mama out the car. Then he grabbed me up in his arms and said those magic words. "How's my princess? I missed ya this much," as he twirled me around. "My, my, ya done growed!"

Now, I was home, I was really home! I ran up the hill as fast as my legs would go, Katherine right behind me. Thea-Thea was coming down the hill to meet us. I jumped up in her arms and laid my head on her neck. *Ohhhhh,* I had missed her so! My Thea-Thea kissed me a thousand times before she let me go in the house looking for my brothers. She gave Katherine a big hug and twirl-around as she let her go to run on down the hill.

My brothers weren't home, but I was going to be glad to see them too. I took my suitcase upstairs and started admiring my new clothes. Me and Katherine grabbed each others' hands and danced around and around. We fell on my bed exhausted with laughter.

Now I said, "Let's see if I can take you to play with *my* friends."

Before, when Katherine was visiting, we were too little to be let loose by ourselves, but now, howdy! howdy! howdy! hoooo!

The family was downstairs, busy meeting and greeting, laughing and talking. I knew not to interrupt grown-ups, so I waited patiently until Thea-Thea saw us standing there, and I asked, "Thea-Thea, can I take Katherine to play with my friends?"

"Ya sho' can—just remember, nothin's changed since ya been gone."

"Yes, ma'am!" I yelled as we ran out the door, down the steps, and down the hill. First I took Katherine to meet Ludie, whom I had told her all about at night while we were lying in bed talking. She was fascinated about what I had told her Ludie had told me about this place she said she was going to go to.

Ludie was sitting on the porch. When she saw me coming, she started crying with joy saying "Oh, ClaraBy, how I've missed you!" We hugged and hugged and hugged. Then she said those famous words, "Where have you been all my life?"

"You've been right here in my heart," I said with tears in my eyes. I introduced Katherine to her.

Katherine said, "I've heard so much about you."

Ludie said, "I can only imagine," smiling. "Come, ClaraBy she said. Sit down, I've written you a poem."

"Oh boy!" I squealed. Ludie was good at writing poems and songs. Katherine and I sat down on the porch at her feet as she read:

> You've been gone from me for a while,
> But I still can see your smile.
> Your voice I still hear,
> Ringing softly in my ear.
> I've been lonely and I've been sad,
> With you away no friend I've had,
> You make me laugh until I cry,
> I will love you until I die.
> *LOVE, TUDDY LUDIE*

"Oh, Ludie," I said softly, "that's beautiful. You wrote that for me?"

"Yes, my little pal, I've really missed you."

"Me too," I said.

She folded the sheet of paper up and gave it a kiss as she handed it to me and told me to keep it.

Katherine and I stayed with her until she got tired. We didn't go anywhere else; we went straight home.

Ludie had the same effect on Katherine as she had on me. We walked slowly and kicked rocks. Talking seriously, Katherine said, "She's so sweet; just like you said."

"I told you so. She's special," I said. "It's as if she's different or something. She makes me feel special too. I love her so."

"Now I really know what you mean when you say she's going to be an angel," Katherine said. "I'm glad I met your special friend."

"Yeah," I said, "me too . . . . *LAST ONE HOME IS A ROTTEN EGG!*" Off we went, running and giggling up the hill.

It was *ON* that night! Uncle Robert was a big spender, so although it was an off-payday weekend, everybody gathered at our house, 'cause it was *par-TAY*-time!

Aunt Idella had loaded the car down with food and other things for Thea-Thea. Thea-Thea fried chicken and made her famous rolls. The house was full, the *homebrew* was ready, and the moonshine was flowing freely.

Big Mama sat in the bedroom by the window crocheting, as if she was plum deaf, rocking back and forth in the big rocking chair. She seemed to be whistling to the music as the others danced all around her. But later we found out that she had totally tuned out the "worldly" music and was whistling "Yield Not to Temptation," as she crocheted.

I remember the story that Thea-Thea would tell us as we sat on the front porch about her childhood days. She said that even though Big Mama "didn't take no stuff" in her younger days, that it was a must that everybody in her house went to church, that included the men who boarded with her. She didn't play when it came to serving the Lord. Thea-Thea told us that going to church, was a way for her and my daddy to sit together during their courting days.

Granddaddy Russell had been killed in a rock fall in the mines when they lived in Virginia. Big Mama had left there with her six children and gone back to North Carolina to live with an aunt. She had overcome a lot of adversities and raised her kids without a man around.

Thea-Thea said she would give you a back hand lick for the slightest disrespect. She also carried a snub-nose in her *hussy bag*, fully loaded, and everybody knew she didn't take no junk.

Well, Thea-Thea said my brother Walter got drunk when he was sixteen years old, and had come home trying to act grown. "Big Mama tol' him go to da big tree out back and get a switch 'cause he was in for a good whooping. He refused, saying he was a *man* now and he wouldn't be taking no whoopings." Thea-Thea was laughing so hard remembering the incident, she could hardly finish telling us the story. She said as she caught her breath, "Well, Big Mama had gone upside his head so hard wit her fist dat he was out cold. She got scared when she couldn't wake him up. But, when he did wake up, partly from being drunk and partly from being cold-cocked, he apologized and never tried dat again. He left home at seventeen and is now a *minister!* Heeeee, heeeee." Thea-Thea said, "Mama had put da fear of *Jesus* in him wit her right hook!

"Dat's one thang ya learned early," she said. "NO BACK TALK—'yes, ma'am; no, ma'am; yes, sir; no, sir.' right or wrong." Thea-Thea went on to say that Big Mama said commandingly, "NOBODY DAT I FEED AN CLOTHE IS GROWN IN MY HOUSE BUT ME! YA GOT DAT, BUSTER?"

She said Uncle Walter was stammering, saying, "Yes, ma'am, Big Mama, yes, ma'am."

"Po' Bro," Thea-Thea said. "He walked around on eggshells trying to do ever'thang he could to please Big Mama. He never drunk nothing else from dat day to dis."

It was like that in our community too: if you misbehaved down the road, any adult would chastise you, and God forbid if they told on you . . . well, you got another whipping at home! Nobody, and I do mean *none of us kids* would misbehave in front of *any* adult, not even the camp drunk.

With the night winding down, the crowd began to wander off one by one. Then it was quiet. Big Mama had given up early and come up stairs to bed. Katherine and I slept in the boys' room in one bed that night, as there were two beds, and Big Mama slept in the other. We played Oh Mary Mack, Mack, Mack and other games while sitting in bed. The boys were on a pallet on the floor at the foot of the beds talking boy talk. Uncle Robert and Aunt Idella slept in my room.

It seemed as if we had just gone to sleep when I heard Daddy stoking up the cook stove, fixing coffee, and talking with Uncle Robert. Soon, the kitchen was busy with Aunt Idella, Big Mama, and Thea-Thea fixing breakfast. Uncle Robert and Daddy had gone to the front porch with their cups of coffee.

After we all had eaten breakfast and the kitchen was clean, Uncle Robert started loading up the car. They were leaving early so as to make it to the evening services at their church. Uncle Robert was head deacon and Aunt Idella sang in the choir.

We hugged and kissed and said our goodbyes. Thea-Thea cried, me and Katherine cried.

My big-head brothers were trying to be *a man* about it. Uncle Robert had given them both a crisp $5.00 bill. They were tickled. They kept popping it until I thought it would surely tear in half, grinning from ear to ear.

I knew it was almost time to start getting ready for Sunday school, so I had gotten my clothes on.

"Well, did you enjoy your vacation?" Thea-Thea asked as she was braiding my hair.

"Oh yes, ma'am, I had big, big fun." I had turned seven years old while I was in Virginia and was now getting ready to enter the second grade. Boy was I excited.

Chapter Twenty-Four

OH BROTHER, YOU KNOW BETTER

My sister had been getting fat again. But I had been too busy with my school work to even wonder about it, until I came home from school one day and Thea-Thea said the stork had come while we were in school and left us a fine baby boy!

Oh boy, I thought, *that darn invisible bird again.* Paula was barely walking! WHAT THE WORLD! WHAT THE WORLD! I wanted to see this bird, 'cause he was leaving these little gremlins in almost every house in the four communities of my world. He was one busy bird, I thought. I wondered how he made them so fast, and in all colors! He must be magic, 'cause while we were walking out of the hollow through the white camp to school one morning, the women were talking across the road to each other about the big bird having left a baby at so-and-so's house last night.

Even Ms. Dotson, who lived up the hollow from us in the next black community, had been "blessed," Thea-Thea said, "by this big bird."

"*I, I* KNOW *I* BEEN CHANGED, *I, I* KNOW *I* BEEN CHANGED, *I, I* KNOW *I* BEEN CHANGED! DA ANGELS IN HEAVEN DONE SIGNED MY NAME." HMMM, HUM, HUM, HUM, HUM . . ." We could hear the people singing as we ran across the hill from our house to Sunday school. Russell had me by the hand, and we ran as fast as we could. Junior was sick, so he had stayed home.

Well, that's a story in itself. No matter what was done on Friday and Saturday, Daddy and Thea-Thea made sure that we were up, dressed, and ready to go to Sunday school. No if, ands, or buts about it; if you lived in this house, you went to Sunday school and church *everrrry* Sunday.

My Thea-Thea kept us dressed nicely all the time. The boys had their special pants, shoes, and shirts that could only be worn on Sundays. She would say to me, "Baby Girl, make sho' whenever ya leave home yo underclothes is nice and clean underneath." So I had to keep my nice undies for special days. They were so pretty and frilly. I even had panties for each day of the week written right on them. I thought I was something, you hear me?

My Thea-Thea was in church every Sunday, no matter how tired and sleepy she may have been. Now Daddy, that's another story; he never went to church. Us kids, huh, we knew we had to go, so we prepared the night before.

Well, you know by now that Russell had no problem with it, but Junior, well, what can I say . . . ? Me, I loved it. I loved the singing most of all.

Thea-Thea's motto was *If you're too sick to go to Sunday school, then you're too sick to go out of the house or off the porch all day.* So we've gone to Sunday school and church many hard days so we wouldn't miss the treat of getting to go to the movies and just plain getting out of the hollow on Sunday evening.

As luck would have it, this particular Sunday, Junior just had to test Thea-Thea by having a stomach ache. We really thought he was sick until around three o'clock when Mr. Judd came by in his truck to pick up the kids, as he always did, and take us down to the movie house and bring us back.

Junior suddenly got well around two o'clock! Running down the steps, he announced, "Thea-Thea, I feel much, much better!"

She replied, "I'm so glad, Junior. I was thanking I was gonna have to call da doctor."

"No, ma'am," Junior said, "I feel pretty good."

Thea-Thea said coyly, "Well, dat's good."

So Junior ran upstairs to get dressed, thinking he was going to get to go to the movies. Heee, heeeeeeee!

As the horn blew up and down the hollow for the kids to be ready when Mr. Judd came back down, Junior came running down the steps, all dressed and ready to go.

Thea-Thea looked at him and said, "Now, just where do ya thank ya going?"

Junior looked as if he was about to descend into the deep as he said, "Uh, I heard Mr. Judd blow and I . . . I . . .

"I what?" replied Thea-Thea. "I know ya don't thank ya gonna go to da movies do ya?"

Junior couldn't answer; he looked like that little dog that roams the road, as he went back upstairs, looking out the window as we all jumped up in the back of the truck with the rest of the kids.

"Where's Junior?," Tim asked Russell.

"He's sick," I said quickly before Russell could answer. "At least, he said he was this morning before church, but then he got all well and Thea-Thea told him to . . . stay . . . sick."

"Hahahahahaha!" Everybody was laughing.

Russell, who was not big on talking said, "That's one rule I wouldn't dare attempt to break, 'cause Thea-Thea don't play when it comes to going to church."

All the kids said, "Amen, it's the same way in my house."

I felt sorry for Junior, but he knew the rule. As we were driving by, J. J. and Sarah were standing on the front porch. I stopped laughing and gave a half wave as my heart ached for them. "One day, I'm gonna save up enough money for them to go with us . . . Yes I am," I thought. They never got to go to the movies, cause their daddy never had any money. My Daddy thought Mr. Monroe was the worst kind of man you could think of. He loved it when they came to eat at the house, cause he felt they were well fed, at least that day.

Chapter Twenty-Five

Bee-Bee and Boo

The little gremlin has turned two and a half years old and is my little shadow, following me everywhere I go. Russell and Junior spoiled the little fat head boy. He is the cutest thing with fat, juicy jaws, laughing all the time.

Little Paula calls me Bee-Bee, and my heart melts. I must admit, she has grown on me. I carry her around on my hip. I even jump red hot pepper rope with her on my hip; she be squealing with glee. I am the red hot pepper, double-dutch rope-jumping queen! And . . . I no longer have my bed to myself, as she stays with me every weekend and all summer—when I'm not visiting my cousin.

Oh, and by the way, my sister is getting fat AGAIN! GEE ALREADY!"

It was a long, cold winter. It seemed as if the snow was above my head. We still had to walk out of the hollow to school and to catch the bus if the county had not announced that there would be no school, so we made it fun.

The big bus coming up the hollow would make deep tracks that we would walk in out of the hollow. By this time, the county had finally built a shed right off the highway for the kids who rode the bus, so we could stand out of the weather.

Sometimes, the weather made it impossible to go to school. Now, those were the days! Sledding down the hill on anything we could, all day long. A big fire was made to keep us warm. But we seemed to be oblivious to the cold.

Time passed so fast I was now in the *third* grade and doing quite well. My teacher said I was one of her best students. I was "the leader type," she said. She let me choose a helper to pass out our lunches, which we bring from home in brown paper bags with our names on them. The bags were greasy from being used day after day after day . . .

Everybody usually had the same thing: a biscuit and a piece of souse meat, ham, or peanut butter and jelly, an apple or orange, and a piece of cake, and sometimes, commodity cheese.

There were times someone wouldn't have any lunch, so we had to share with them. It always made me sad to see Sarah and J. J. They almost always had no lunch. I told Thea-Thea about it, and she started packing an extra sandwich or two so that I could give it to them.

Their daddy worked in the mines, but he seemed to not take good care of his family. Daddy used to call him a "sorry rascal." He would say, "A man who don't take care of his family is da worst thang in da world. Dem chilluns didn't ask to be here." He was not allowed to come to our house when they had card games or parties or anything. Daddy told him that his money wasn't welcome in this house and neither was his sorry butt. He would say in a very loud and clear voice, "Go buy yo wife some decent shoes and buy some food for dem chilluns." Then Daddy would mumble under his breath, "a worthless piece of shit . . . got a good woman too." He would shame him every chance he got.

Thea-Thea told Daddy that Ms. AnnaBelle had been ailing a little and was looking a little puny. "A good hard wind will blow her away," she said.

Daddy said, "Yeah, she looks a little blue, and sadder than usual. Dat sorry man of hers needs to be took out an hoss-whipped. I don't know how she put up wit it, but I guess she can't do nothin' bout it wit dem kids . . . . But I sho' as hell would leave his sorry butt if'n I was her."

"But boy, can she sang!" Thea-Thea said. She seemed to be thinking, *Putting all things aside, everybody makes mistakes, some make stupid ones; dat's felt deep down, so now her songs reflect her regrets*. Thea-Thea sighed real heavy and said, "Da Lawd knows, da Lawd knows . . ." And then she brightened up, saying, "She lights up da church every Sunday. Daddy; ya know, she got some of da kids together to form a choir. ClaraBy is leading da first song, 'Tell Da Angels.' Daddy, ya ought to hear dat girl sang. Ain't no music but, they don't need none, 'cause dem girls sanging background is sanging—ya hear me, *sanging, 'Huma-lanka-lanka-lank,*'" she mimicked laughingly. "Man, when she sangs, da whole church is shouting. She walks da aisle at seven years old! You gotta go some Sunday and hear yo child sang," she said.

Daddy was grinning from ear to ear, saying, "Dat's my baby! Dat's my princess."

I thought I was something, child, all this bragging about me.

Ms. Nellie would tell Thea-Thea, "Dat child is gonna make ya some money one of dese days wit dat voice of hers. She ain't shame of nothin'. She throws dat head back and bellows like a cow. Haaaa, haaaa, haaaaaaaa," she'd squeal. "I git such a kick outa her sanging, I tell ya."

Thea-Thea would say, "Lawd, I sho' hope so, but ya know, it's tough out there for us coloreds, dat life ain't no life a'tall."

Our little choir got better and better as time went on. We thought we were something. The *Caravans* maybe!

Chapter Twenty-Six

WHAT THE WORLD, WHAT *THE WORLD!*

It was Saturday evening around six o'clock. It was the off-payday, so money was low. The men had had their fill of *spirits*, and the Crow Pole crowd was winding down. Some had already left, and just a few remained when up the hollow came a *police car!*

I was sitting on the porch with Ludie; so we could see wayyyyyy down the road.

Ludie said, "Oh my," when we heard a siren start up as it topped the small hill at the first house.

By now, all eyes and ears were perked, and every screen door flew open as every porch filled with curious onlookers when the car stopped in front of Aunt Cellie's house. The back door of the police car opened, and out stepped Aunt Cellie.

She threw her head back proudly and said to the two police officers, "Thank ya kindly" as she smoothed her uniform down and slammed the door.

The police car went up the road, turned around at the Crow Pole, and went on down the road, leaving us all with our mouths wide open in amazement, wondering, "WHAT THE WORLD? WHAT THE *WORLD*?!"

Thea-Thea was halfway down the hill as soon as she realized it was Aunt Cellie that was in the police car. Screaming at the top of her lungs, she said, "CELLIE, CELLIE, ARE YA ALL RIGHT?"

Aunt Cellie was half running toward Thea-Thea. "Oh shoot, child," she said, laughing at Thea-Thea, "I'm fine! I just had a little run-in wit da law."

"What kinda run in wit da law?" Thea-Thea said.

"Well . . ." Aunt Cellie said, "let's go to da house, and I'll tell ya all about it. Every nose in the camp is wondering. I'll just let 'em wonder for a while," she said as she started to trot and snicker softly to Thea-Thea. "Girlllllll," she said, "wait till I tell ya what happened!"

Thea-Thea said excitedly, trying to keep up with her, "WHAT? WHAT!"

"I need a good stiff, and I do mean a good STIFFFF drank," Aunt Cellie said as she ran up the steps.

Daddy had left the Crow Pole and was walking up the hill as I ran to join him.

They gathered at the kitchen table, and with a stiff drink of moonshine, Aunt Cellie began to tell them what had happened. Being unnoticed, I stayed in the bedroom so I could really get a good ear full.

Now, most of the women in our communities worked for the *affluent white people,* and Aunt Cellie worked for Mr. and Mrs. Abernathy. She had worked for them for several years.

She caught her breath and started by saying:

> Well, Ms. Abernathy had done gone shopping wit da kids, leaving only me and Mr. Abernathy in da house. I was standing at da sink washing up da dishes after I had done served lunch.
>
> All of a sudden, I feels somebody come up behind me and pin me to da sink. He had both hands over my breast and was bumping away. Well, I was washing out da cast iron skillet dat I had just fixed the steak in; so I just lifted it over my head and *lam-bammed* him over da head a couple of times. He was bleeding like a stuffed pig as he fell back against da table.

Girlllll, I tell ya, I was scared to death. I didn't know what to do then.

He let out a yell and a string of cuss words, saying he was gonna have me 'rested.

Well, I was scared I tell ya! He was bleeding like a stuffed hog—and wouldn't shut up! He ran to da phone and called da police!

I was saying "Please Mr. Abe, let me help ya!"

"Don't touch me!" he screamed as he called me all kinda names, and saying I was always trying to *tempt* him by wearing my uniforms too tight!

Well, I got pissed then and told him I wore 'em like he bought 'em, and if I "tempted" him, he had no damn biss-ness looking, 'cause he was not my cup of tea, and nothin' 'bout him gave me a tingle, "so dat's on you, buddy, and if ya ever touch me again, I'll slap all hell outa ya!"

I don't know what else I said I was so mad just thinking of dat slimy dog looking at me in dat way.

I couldn't run 'cause I knew dat would look bad on me, 'cause blood and water was all ov'r me, on da back of my uniform. So I stayed by da door til da police came, which seemed to take forever!

Da sorry SOB told 'em dat he had caught me stealing . . . I called him a damn lie, and he slapped me right in front of da police.

Well, he just shouldna . . . I doubled my fist up and gave him one cross his lips as hardddd as I could!

Da police grabbed me then, and I started crying and telling 'em what had happened. They turned me loose as I screamed, "He was feeling me!" He tried to lie out of it, but da police officers said dat he should just forget about it and fire me, 'cause if da missus fount out what had happened, he might be in trouble *again*!

I screamed, "Again! Again?!"

Well, da cop was ho-humming around, trying not to let da cat outa da bag. As it turns out, he had done da same thang to another one of da helpers from down da road, wit almost da same report, and had paid her to keep her mouth shut. So this time, he had met his match!

"Let it go, Abernathy," they said. "Ya know ya got a reputation for this kinda thang; so if ya wanta salvage yo marriage, ya had better not let da Mrs. hear 'bout this one. The best thing for ya to do is think of a real good *lie* to tell yo" Mrs. about yo head and why yo help ain't coming back no mo.

The fat cop said, "I ain't having nothin' to do wit this one, buddy, you on yo own. You know da Mrs. gonna put two and two together—she ain't da stupid one—but if she stays wit yo perverted ass, I'll have to rethink it."

"Well, da sorry SOB had da nerve to tell me I was fired. I told him, like hell I am! I quit!" And I said, "I will be back for my damn money, and ya had better have a bonus in it for me—don't she gonna know 'bout her friend next door too!" I screamed as the police officers' faces turned three shades of red.

Da big burly one spoke up and said, "Oh Lawd, Abernathy, pay her now! Pay her right now! I don't give a flying fish what you tell da wife!"

He reached in his back pocket, pulled out his billfolder, and threw a hand fulla bills at me.

I looked at him wit da look of pure Satan, but I picked 'em up, 'cause I saw some *hunda-dollah* bills in da pile! Heeeeee heeee heeee. I weren't 'bout to give 'em up . . . I's well compensated for dat *feel* he got!.

Aunt Cellie and Thea-Thea fell out laughing as she pulled the bundle out of her brassiere. They were counting and laughing.

"Oh my goooodnessssss!" screamed Aunt Cellie. "It's seven hunda dollahs here!" Jumping up and down and turning all around, waving the money in her hands, she said, "I DON'T GIVE A FLYING FISH WHAT HE TELLS DAAAA MIIIIISSSSSUUUSSSSS! HEEE HEEEEEEE!"

Daddy was up pacing the floor by now, mad as a rabid dog, clenching and unclenching his fists, slamming his fist in his hand.

"Our womens ain't never been safe 'round 'em for years and years and years, and be damned if it gonna happen right under my nose! I's got a good mind to—"

"NO! NO! Cal, don't git in no trouble!" Thea-Thea screamed. "Ya don't stand a chance against da law round here, ya know dat. Why, they'd just soon as lynch some of ya as look at ya. Look at dat boy down south they found in dat river. *Please, Cal*, just calm down," she said as she gathered him in her arms.

I heard Daddy say, "Dat sorry SOB. I proud of ya Cellie for stickin' up fo yo'self. I'd be in jail *or hell* now if dat hada been HoneyBabe."

"Hee, hee, heeeee, I wonder how he's gonna explain his head to da 'missus'!" said Aunt Cellie.

She was one happy camper as she continued to tell Daddy and Thea-Thea more of the juicy details . . .

"Some of da neighbors was on they porches as we came out da front door, but not da little tippy toe next door. I know they wondering what happened, or already done figgr'd it out."

"He's gonna have a hard time keeping his lie straight, 'cause da *Mrs.* KNOWS I don't steal. Why, she done left money and little pieces of jewelry laying round deliberately, I know, just to see if I'd take it. I always played dumb as a donut, 'cause ya know ya can't let 'em know ya got a brain. I would always say all dumb like 'Ah, Ms., I found this laying here or there.' She would always say guiltily, 'Oh, I must have dropped it!' I'd say to myself, *Yeah, right*. Then I'd say, 'You's gonna havta' be mo' car'ful. Ya don't want da mister to fuss at ya.'

"'Sure, Cellie,' she'd say, 'You right. I'll be more careful.' She finally stopped after a while. I feel sorry for her in a way she tries to be so perfect in *everythang* an fails badly. He orders her around an so do da chilluns. Neither he nor da chilluns respect her. Da only respect she gits is from me.

"I always tried to respect him as my boss, but I always had bad vibes 'bout him, now I knows why. If I got my hunches right, da 'Mrs.' probably knows da truth wit out saying.

"'Fore we left out da door, one of da cops said, 'Ahhh Ms., I advise ya to kinda keep this quiet, as we don't want no trouble . . . you know what I mean?'

"I had to hold my piece 'fore I go off and end up in jail 'cause my head jerked round so fast I almost got a crook fixing to spew out da hatred I had for such varmints dat was standing in front of me. I was thanking 'bout da hunda of years us colored girls and women had to put up wit this CRAP, and keep our mouths shut! I had to catch myself and squinch my butt cheeks tight to keep from saying what I really wanted to say. So I just said, 'Yeah,' with a big smirk on my face, 'I know just exactly what ya mean.' Don't worry, I don't think I havta say a word.' I looked at him wit a look of pure disgust as I said again, 'I ain't gonna have to say a *word*.'

"I thank he got my message from da look on my face. *A red-faced bastard,* I thought."

"'Ah, can we offer ya a ride home, ma'am?' da short puggy officer said kindly, jerking me back to reality.

"'Sho'', I said proudly, 'do dat.' I wondered to myself, *now how's dat gonna look?* But they didn't want me walking home wit my uniform all bloody. They knowed there was people in da white camp I had to pass through that knowed me and they might ask questions."

Well. Big Sis and the kids, Ms. Noon, Ms. Nellie, Ms. Francine, and Ms. Niddy couldn't stand it any longer, and up the hill they came. Daddy took his pipe and went out on the front porch. They laughed and talked for hours as Aunt Cellie told them the story of what had happened, demonstrating every move.

Mrs. Nellie said, "Shiiiitt, for dat kinda money, I'da let dat old bastard cop a feel myself!" They all fell out laughing and talked way up in the night. I had the kids in my room playing, and finally, we laid down and fell asleep.

Chapter Twenty-Seven

THE FUNERAL

Russell had been getting restless lately. He wasn't that into school anymore. He and Junior talked a lot lately about the future. He would tell Junior that he wanted to see the world.

Junior had asked him what did he want to see, and Russell replied that he wanted to go to different parts of the world. Russell said that he didn't want no part of the coal mines . . . Junior said, "Me neither. I have seen enough now with Oscar losing his finger!"

"Yeah," Russell said, "that very well could have meant his life if he hadn't been quick."

"Yeah," Junior said, "I know; that's what worries me about Daddy. He's not as active as he used to be, and I've noticed he's not as strong sometimes."

"Yeah," Russell said, "he seems to cough a lot."

"Yeah," Junior said, "and he don't breathe so good either."

"Yeah," said Russell. "You know, Junior, that old well is about petered out, and water is getting mighty scarce. Lord only knows what's going to happen if the coal company doesn't get on the ball with the project they've been working on."

"Yeah," Junior replied, "I don't think they will run a line upon this hill. Do you?"

"Well, it would be a pretty big job," Russell said. "But you know what, they could run a line to the roadway leading up to our yard, and we could make it from there."

"Yeah, that would be a help. At least it wouldn't be so far away like the well is now," said Russell, looking as if he could visualize it.

Then he said, "I want to go and find something better, so I can be a help to Daddy and Thea-Thea. They deserve a good life. Maybe move out of this hollow into a more convenient place."

"Yeah . . ." Junior said softly. "They love this hollow, though; it will be hard to get them out of here."

"I know," said Russell, "but you can see, the way things are going, there's change coming, whether we want it or not."

After a long, hard day at school, I moped into the house and threw my books on the steps and headed for the kitchen. My big brother Oscar was sitting at the kitchen table with his hand bandaged up almost to his elbow.

I screamed, "Bro, what happened?!"

He tried to set me on his knee with his good hand and explain, as I sobbed and sobbed.

"I'm all right, Baby Girl," he said.

One of his fingers had been cut off at work. He was telling Daddy and Thea-Thea how blessed he was that it was not his whole hand. He had been taken to the hospital, treated, and released. He had kept his finger in a large match box. I begged him for it so that I could give it a proper burial. He stayed at the house longer that evening than usual.

After supper, I asked if I could tell Pearlie, Olive, Sarah, and J. J. to help me bury it. Well, to give it a proper burial, we had to have a little church before the burial. We started shouting, and singing, having a real home-going good time in front of the outhouse. J. J. was the preacher; I was the singer, Pearlie, Sarah and Olive were the shouting audience. We had church, you hear me! We marched from the porch to the front of the outhouse, where I had placed some chairs for us to sit in. J. J. was the pallbearer *and* preacher.

Walking slowly behind him, I sang, "When We All Get to Heaven, What a Day of Rejoicing That Will Be." Olive had brought her tambourine.

Olive and Sarah shouted all the way to the chairs and sat down. J. J. preached hummm-ma, and a hummmm-ma, wiping his brow with a white rag, pacing back and forth.

Finishing the sermon I started to sing "In the Sweet Bye and Bye, We Shall Meet on That Beautiful Shore." We marched around to the back of the outhouse where J.J. had dug a hole for the grave. J.J. carrying the box, hands it to me and I laid the match box in the hole as I had a fainting, farting, falling out last cry.

We shook hands and parted to our different homes singing, "I'll Fly Away, Oh Glory, I'll Fly Away." Olive beat her tambourine all the way down the hill singing to the top of her lungs, glad she could get out on a school evening.

MY BUDDIES AND ME

My friends and I were always up in the woods during the spring and summer months when the paw-paws and blackberries were ripe, and in the fall when the *hickle nuts,* as we called them, fell to the ground. It seemed as if we never encountered any dangerous critters. We had discovered this tree that from where we stood seemed to reach the sky and we were all fascinated by it.

So one Saturday, since I had the skinny on where heaven was, I convinced my friends J. J., Olive, Sarah, Pearlie and Buster to follow me up the mountain to that big, tall tree that seemed to be touching the sky so that we could go have a little talk with Jesus about my friend Ludie, 'cause the saints said, "Just a Little Talk with Jesus Makes It Right."

Well, off we went climbing and climbing and climbing. Our folks had no idea that we were on this Christian journey. We were going to *surprise* them when we returned with the GOOD NEWS.

We left around noon I guess, give or take. Now it was getting late, and we still had not reached that tree, which could no longer be seen. J. J. was whining "ClaraBy, I'm tired and thirsty . . ."

"Yeah, me too, replied Sarah, and hungry too."

Olive just kept repeating, "Som'pin told me not to come, Granny's gonna kill me, som'pin told me, I shoulda listened, but noooooo, not me," she said sorrowfully.

Buster just nodded his head in agreement.

At this time, I am lost for words which is unusual, as I was feeling the same hunger pains and thirst at this time.

"When we gon' git there?" asked Buster.

"ClaraBy, I'm gitting scared," said Olive.

"Yeah, how we gon' git back down from heaven if they close 'fore we git there?" asked Sarah.

"Don't be silly," Olive said boldly, "heaven *never* closes."

Buster said puzzled, "Well, how we know Jesus ain't somewhere else today?"

"Yeah says Pearlie, He might be."

Mind you, we are six to eight years old, off to conquer the world. Not enough sense between us to make good sense.

My head was turning from left to right as one after the other said something. I finally said, "I think it's just a little ways more."

Thank you, LORD, for looking out for stupid children such as us. Because, we were lost, and I do mean lost. After listening to their whining and worrying, I began to worry too. Now I'm thinking, *What if something jumps out at us?*

Nerves were getting to all of us, when I suddenly said, "*Ruuuunnnnnn!*"

We all took off running for our lives, as my nerves had gotten the best of me, and I thought I heard something coming. We ended up going down the wrong way, having to fight off briars and bushes. Moving was slow, and we were scared to death.

Olive was praying out loud now, and I was saying my goodnight prayer, "Now I lay me down to sleep . . ."

Pearlie, Sarah and Buster were crying; Olive was praying; J. J. and I were ahead leading the way to nowhere . . . and it was approaching dusk.

Olive was thoroughly convinced that if not eaten by a bear, her grandmother was gonna finish her off. Now, reality and paranoia were beginning to set in as I began to think I could hear, my Thea-Thea calling my name.

"*Listen!*" I shouted.

We all stopped dead and listened. Nothing, absolutely no sound but crickets, frogs, and only God knows what other sounds those were.

Now we're all crying, when suddenly, we heard "CLARA-BYYY! OOOOLIVE! JAAAYYYY JAAAYYY!, SARAAAAHHH! BUUUUSTERRRR! PEARLIEEEE!

They were coming! They were coming for us! Junior was leading the pack! Hallelujah! Hallelujah! There is a God and He is home all of the time!

Needless to say, we had to pay by the seat of our pants, but it was worth it. My friends didn't speak to me for a day or so. After that, we laughed about it and teased each other as to who was the most scared and such.

Poor Olive got the worst punishment, as suspected. After the beat-down we all got, and the threat of never to do it again, Olive had to endure seeing us play up and down the road as she sat on the porch or passed in the car on their way to church.

She was not to play with us ever again it seems in life, especially with me. I wouldn't dare go to visit her, as I was thought to be the culprit that yielded her to temptation.

Chapter Twenty-Eight

THE UNCLE I NEVER KNEW

Russell was out on the front porch one evening talking with Daddy. They were deep in conversation. As it turned out, Russell was telling Daddy that he wanted to join the army. He promised Daddy that he would finish his education no matter what. My daddy said if that was his choice, then he'd let him go.

It was hard for Thea-Thea. She cried and cried. "YA AIN'T OLD ENOUGH YET!" she cried. "Ya too young to leave home!" she screamed. "Ya might get hurt, and who gonna see after ya?!"

She finally quieted down long enough to take a deep breath and said, "Oh Lawd, please watch over my boy." She sobbed softly.

My daddy was so proud of him. He gave him his pocket watch, the one thing that we all knew he treasured, as he said that his brother had given it to him when he had turned sixteen and ready to face the world.

Daddy said he was about nine years or so he thinks, when his brother had left to join the army, and he had never heard from him again.

"Cal! Thea-Thea said, You never told me dat!"

"I know, HoneyBabe," Daddy said, I just never did."

He never knew his father, and his mother had died in childbirth. He and his brother John were raised by an aunt, who was their daddy's sister. He said, "If ya could call it raisin'. We just existed til each of us could git old enough to git away. John said he coming back to git me, but he never did."

We didn't know any of Daddy's family. *We* were his family, all he had in this world. He said, "After my brother left, I didn't know where he went or whether he dead or live." He looked so forlorn.

He had simply told Thea-Thea that he didn't have any family.

So off Russell went to join the army. Daddy and Thea-Thea put his age up and signed for him to go in. Thea-Thea did it with trembling hands and pride.

Junior and I got to stay home from school the day Russell was going off to boot camp. Mr. Tibbs came and got us. We went to the bus station downtown.

There were seventeen boys boarding the bus all together. There were three other black boys with Russell, all going to Fort Jackson, South Carolina, to boot camp.

I saw this sign with this white man on it that said he was "Uncle Sam." I wondered which side of the family he was from. I studied the picture with great care. Then I thought, he could be on Thea-Thea's side of the family 'cause there were some darn-near white people down in Virginia on Big Mama's side of the family, and I do mean darn-near-white. Aunt Esther was a tiny little white woman, but she *wasn't* white. Well, you couldn't tell by looking; I just knew she was Big Mama's baby sister. Then there was Aunt Rose, who had *blonde* kinky hair and very rosy cheeks and white—now something is wrong with this picture if she ain't white, but she wasn't.

This mixed-blood thing was blowing my mind, but I settled for the fact that *Uncle Sam* had to be on my Big Mama's side of the family, and being as he was family, he would certainly take care of his own flesh-and-blood nephew . . . .

Russell and Junior were deep in conversation off to themselves, while I studied the picture that the sergeant was standing beside.

I walked over close to them and heard Russell tell Junior to take care of "his two girls" now that he was the other man in the house. Russell made him promise that he would finish high school. They hugged and walked back over to Daddy and Thea-Thea who was boo-hooing. Russell gave her a big hug and told her not to worry. He boarded the bus after kissing me and telling me to be good.

He gave Daddy a handshake, and then grabbed him and hugged him tight. Daddy had tears in his eyes as the bus pulled away. Everyone was quiet as we returned home. I missed him so much, but I was so proud of him.

Chapter Twenty-Nine

CHANGE GONNA COME

Junior, well, he's still in school . . . for now, and I'm finally riding that great big yellow bus. WHEEE!

My first day on that bus was amazing. I had never ever experienced anything like it in my whole entire ten years.

It was incredible to look out the window and see the houses go by. Stopping and starting at every railroad crossing, hollering to Mr. Luster, "it's all clear on this side, and it's all clear on this side too!"

"Thanks, Mr. Luster would say, y'all sho a big help."

"You're welcome Mr. Luster," we all would chant.

I was quite excited to be a big girl now, so I was determined to dig into my lessons, and try very hard to make good grades. I had good report cards that had shown my hard work had paid off. I had made A's, and B's all through my first years of school. Ludie would help me if I had any problems I couldn't solve. Even though she was too sick to go to school, she was very, very smart.

Now the little town where we lived was full—and I do mean full—of *black* people. They came from all points of the deep, deep South to this little town. They were in almost every hollow, nook, and cranny of every community in this little county.

When I got to the new school, there were boys and girls I had never ever seen before. Nor did I know they even existed, and so many of them! Junior had told me, but I wasn't prepared; being so excited during the summer just thinking about going on that big bus was all I thought about.

Junior had said, "Now, Baby Girl, it ain't nothing compared to the big school that I'm gonna be going to soon. *They got some pretty little girls there, and I'm a'gonna git me one,"* he sang off key.

"Yeah, right," I said, "you won't even talk to girls."

"I mighta used to won't, but I'm gonna now," he said, patting me on the head.

"Junior, how do you know about the big school? You don't go there."

"Un-huh," he said, Mr. Cross took the whole eight grade there on the bus for a science project, and a walk-through . . . . You know what Baby Girl?"

"What?" I asked.

"I'm beginning to believe what Big Mama says about you."

"Yeah, what's that?"

"That you been here before," thumping me lightly on the head as he ran out the door yelling, Thea-Thea, I'm going to play football with the guys."

"Okay, she replied, but be careful—y'all boys play too rough."

"Ahhh, you worry too much, I'm gonna play on the big team when I get to high school," he said as he took the steps two at a time, twirling the football around in his hands.

* * *

Well, as life goes, the year passed with not much fanfare. School was *out!"* I ran all the way up the hollow to show my Thea-Thea and Daddy my report card. Junior was lagging behind, as usual. He had not done so very good, but not so very bad either—at least he had passed.

So next school term, he would be going to the big high school. When he handed Daddy his report card, Daddy handed it to Thea-Thea as he could not read or write, so Thea-Thea told Daddy what Junior's report card said and what it meant. (My Thea-Thea could read and write 'cause she had gone through the fourth grade.)

Daddy told Junior, "Well, son, just keep up da good work. *Mother-wit,* son, *mother-wit* is what ya gotta have. Ya know I can't read nor write, but ya don't have to be no genius, just try yo best and life will pay off for ya."

"Yeah, Junior, I said excitedly, I'll help you!"

Junior said, "Thanks, Baby Girl," as he ran upstairs, thankful that he had not gotten a tongue-lashing or worse. It made him feel even more like trying. He promised them that he would do better, and he said, "I told Russell that I would finish school, and I am, and then who knows? Maybe I'll go to the army myself." He was glowing as he thought of his future.

Chapter Thirty

HEAR NO EVIL, SEE NO EVIL

I stayed home this summer to help Big Sis and Thea-Thea. The mines had been slow all year. There seemed to be more strikes going on all over the county causing the mines to be closed until matters were resolved.

Mr. Ed, our neighbor who lived in the house across from us on the hill, had more time at home and more time to be whooping on Ms. Viv, his wife. It seemed as if that was our weekly entertainment. Mr. Ed and Ms. Viv fighting; well, Ms. Viv wasn't doing the fighting, she was getting beat up. They drank all the time, seven days a week. I don't know how he kept a job, but he worked every day.

Ms. Viv had drunk so much and been beat so much that she staggered even when she wasn't drunk. She was sweet as she could be and would give you anything; it just seemed as if that was their enjoyment, drinking and fighting. Nobody meddled in their business though; if they fought, nobody said a word; they just let them fight, or rather, just let Mr. Ed beat Ms. Viv.

Being kids, we thought it was funny. We sort of looked forward to it. She would curse up a storm at Mr. Ed, who barely said anything until he got tired and then it didn't take much to set him off. We think she had gotten so used to it she thought that was his way of showing her he loved her.

One afternoon, on one of the days that the mines were down, Mr. Ed was heard hollering at Ms. Viv.

"Hey, Viv, fix me some chittlins."

"I ain't got no chittlins," she replied.

"Den git some," he said.

Ms. Viv started down the hill and down the road to the company store. Soon after, she came back with the chitterlings.

Thea-Thea said they were frozen solid and were suppose to be thawed out and then cleaned.

Well, Ms. Viv being as she is, simply let them thaw out enough to come out of the bucket and dumped them in a big pot on the stove. They took hours to cook and were swimming in grease and other things. Well, needless to say, Ms. Viv got a whooping she'll never forget and neither will any of us that heard it.

Still, no one intervened, but nobody—and I do mean nobody—was laughing. It sounded like the windows were rattling with him knocking her this way and that. If she started for the door, he would drag her back inside. This seemed to go on forever. But nobody—and I do mean *nobody*—said anything.

Ms. Nellie came out on her back porch and looked up the hill, shook her head, and went back in the house.

Thea-Thea was in the kitchen sitting at the table. Just sitting there, not saying a word, with her hands folded and her head bowed. Daddy was sitting out on the back porch, which was unusual. I was upstairs in my window listening at Ms. Viv scream. But nobody intervened and nobody said a word.

It seemed as if it was an unspoken *right* that was accepted. I didn't understand it; I just knew I wanted to go over there and stop him, but . . . *I'm just a little girl*, I thought.

The same thing had happened up the hollow in the last white camp with another couple that drank all the time. It was said that Mr. Wilkinson had told Ms. Molly Wilkinson time and time again that he was gonna "blow her frigging head off" if she didn't do this or that, and was always beating on her and the kids. *Nobody ever intervened.*

Finally, late one Saturday night, he actually did pull the trigger and blew her chest out. Then he killed himself.

Mr. Man came knocking late that Saturday night with the news. He was visibly shaken as he told Thea-Thea and Daddy the bad news. By that time, the whole camp was wide awake with the news. Thea-Thea put on a pot of coffee as they were talking.

Me and Junior were upstairs in his room over the vent, listening intently. His vent is over the kitchen where the talk was being done. Then my big brothers, Oscar and Frank, came in the door. They had gone up to the house where the tragedy had taken place as soon as they got the news. They both lived close to the house.

Frank said he never wanted to see anything like that again ever. They were upset talking about the scene.

It was not something I wanted to keep listening to, so I didn't bother to listen anymore. My brother had the vent all to himself, as I went to bed wondering what would happen to the boys, Little Jeff and Todd.

I never went up past that house when I went to play with Janice. We would look at the house from a distance. It was an empty, lonely-looking, spooky house. Somebody came and took the boys after that, and we never found out where they went. Jeff and Todd, I'll never forget them. They always looked broken . . . and lonely. They would play with us until their dad found them playing with the colored children and dragged them away, kicking and screaming, as he cursed and fussed at them for playing with us.

Well, Ms. Viv survived the beat-down but not without permanent scars and broken bones. She was black-and-blue all over, with a broke arm and jaw. Mr. Ed cried and cried, drunk as a skunk. The more he looked at what he had done, the more he drank, trying to block it out of his mind. Ms. Viv just drank, never acknowledging her wounds.

It seems as if after that, they slowed down a little bit and only drank on the weekends, still fighting, just not as violently and not nearly as often, until one day, it seemed as if it had been forever since we had heard them fighting.

Chapter Thirty-One

A Whole New World

So when school started again after the exciting summer we had, Junior began really digging into his homework instead of playing and half doing it. We studied together, and after a while, Junior was helping me instead of me helping him—ain't that a crock, I thought I was the smart one.

My first-year experience in the new school had been somewhat uneventful in that being a fifth grader, we were sort of nonexistent to the upper grades and pretty much pampered by the six-graders knowing what they had gone through the year before.

Our fifth grade classroom was off to itself and we were virtually left to ourselves except for coming and going. So I had dug into my school work making straight A's. We only played with each other during recess, so we had gotten to know each other very well. Olive, Pearlie, Buster and I were all in the same grade together with all of the other kids from different places. We had made it fun together, and met new friends.

Ludie was so excited when I'd tell her every detail about the new experience of being on the bus and the new school. She would say, "Oh, ClaraBy, how I wish I could go to school just once more."

"Oh, Ludie, you ain't missing much," I'd say, trying not to make her feel so bad. It broke my heart to know that she would never, never get to go to school or anything else that was fun. She had been dealt a "dirty hand," which was the phrase the card players would say at the games when their cards didn't look so good. Only, Ludie couldn't do anything about it, and neither could I, and . . . and . . . it made me cry.

"Oh, ClaraBy, don't cry, please don't cry," said Ludie as she would try to cheer up for me. "I want to know everything you do—that way, I can imagine what it's like. "You see, I live through you. You're my only source of life outside of this house. So I want to know everything that goes on, good and bad. You hear me?" she said as she held me by my shoulders.

"Okay, Ludie, I said, sucking up my tears, okay."

Meanwhile, the men were having angry talks about the mines. How things were going in that arena seemed to be on everyone's mind in every mine camp.

Chapter Thirty-Two

Halfway (completely different)

We are at the halfway point in our schooling, and in the sixth grade. We were like being let out into a whole new world at school. Last year, the new kids that I met seemed nice enough. Our recess time had been spent only with our grade so we had become good playmates and friends. This year, it was completely different. I was used to the kids from the other communities in my class from last year, but this year . . . well, you could see how some of them thought they were *all that*. Some of them had attitudes, I do mean *AT-TI-TUDES!*

Some of the girls thought they were the queen bees, being "high yellow." They would throw their braided hair around, thinking they were all that *and* a bag of chips. Well, I can tell you what I thought they were a bag of . . . but I'll let you figure it out, 'cause I know you know what I mean: "good yellow gone to waste."

So I was kind of laid back, playing with the kids I was familiar with. But I was raised up in the hollow and taught by my brothers as well as my Thea-Thea and Daddy, *not to take no junk*. Don't take no junk? That means don't take no *shhh* . . . stuff."

That's exactly what my Big Sis told me, and I didn't. I was every bit the size of a little pea, but I had a big mouth, and in the hollow, I didn't back down. I'd make you think I was gonna kick your butt, but I was glad a lot of the time that I wasn't challenged, especially from those Simmons girls . . .

They were quiet, big, and dark, with very pretty faces and long hair. They were almost full Indian, and they didn't need to say anything: you just knew not to mess with them. But I really liked them especially Janice, who was one of my best friends. She took me under her wing and made no bones about having my back. She was two years older than me. So I wasn't worried about *nobody* messing with me.

OH NO, NOT AGAIN!

Early, one Saturday morning before daybreak . . . "Thea-Thea, Thea-Thea, *come quick!"*

Mr. Man was on the front porch banging on the door, screaming at the top of his lungs. His face was still covered with black dust, as he had not yet bathed. Thea-Thea jumped out of bed, throwing on her coat, hat, and shoes, even her apron. I was right behind her.

She turned and said, "Get back in there, girl, you can't go," as she grabbed the flashlight off the dresser and flew out the door.

"What the world? What the world!" I thought. Then I saw Ms. Nibby and Ms. Thomas, who was this real old lady, with something in her hand, gitting it up the road to my sister's house, her flashlight moving quickly about in the dark. Shortly after, a car pulled up, with the occupant getting out hastily. I couldn't tell who that was . . . .

I was curious about all the fuss, and nervous. Daddy never moved a muscle. Junior was still snoring. But noooo, not me, I've got ears like ah . . . well whatever animal can hear real good, so I was wide awake at the first scream Mr. Man let out.

My sister had been getting bigger and bigger again, and I had overheard Daddy telling Thea-Thea one day sitting on the porch. "Here she comes, HoneyBabe. I believe she be knocked up again. Umh, umh, umh, every time he hang his pants," Daddy said sadly.

Big Sis was coming up the hill with one on her hip and the others trailing. She looked bewildered. Well, by now, I was a little bit more informed than before, as I was in the middle school now, and you know, talk gets around.

So when Thea-Thea finally came out on the porch and hollered across the road to Ms. Nellie that the stork had arrived finally and brought another beautiful little girl, I thought, *Yeah right, stork my ass.* Oh well, I kept my knowledge to myself, as I was only ten and a half now, and still a little princess in my daddy's eyes, so I had to play the role. A white man is coming out of the house behind Thea-Thea, with a little bag in his hand that I recognized as being Dr. Austin. "Oh my, I thought."

Thea-Thea called for me to come down to the house after a while, and lo and behold, there was another little gremlin lying in my sister's arms, and Mr. Man was grinning like a chess cat. My sister said she was tired. I went over to the bed and started to cry.

"Why are you crying Baby Girl?"

"I don't know Big Sis; I just don't want you to be sick, and it seems like you going to Baby land wears you out."

"Oh, Baby Girl, I'm all right. I'll be good as new 'fore long."

"Yeah-boy, she'll bounce back in no time! She's strong, and healthy," said the dummy I was still not on first-name basis with.

"I looked at him with disgust. I wanted so bad to reach up and pull that damn thing he called a nose right off his face. But I kept my cool. I wasn't feeling him at this moment at all. (*A big watermelon head dummy*) I thought.

Chapter Thirty-Three

LOOKING FOR LOVE

"NELLEEEEEEE!" Thea-Thea hollered from the front porch.

"YEAH?" yelled Ms. Nellie.

"I got a bushel and a half of beans! Come help me snap 'em," said Thea-Thea.

"Okay!" said Ms. Nellie.

Well, that was just good enough this beautiful morning after the men had gone to work. Up the hill they came, Ms. Nellie, Ms. Noon, and Aunt Cellie. They snapped and gossiped about this and that.

"Uh-oh, here she comes," Ms. Nellie said.

It was Ms. Minnie stomping up the hill, dressed to kill in every color you could think of from head to toe. Everybody knew she was a little touched upstairs, so she was looked after and checked on often, as was Ms. Maxwell, because they lived alone and were widows. She was about eighty years old and very spry. Her husband, Mr. Bo, had died several years back, and she was always looking for a man.

"Hi ya, gals?" she asked loudly.

"Fine, Ms. Minnie, hi you doing today?" they all replied. They knew what her answer was going to be, so they all answered the same thing, at the same time as she said, "Oh, child; I's be looking for a man, a good man."

"Yes, ma'am, Ms. Minnie, we know," they replied.

Ms. Minnie kept right on talking: "Not no handsome man, a good man; not no tall man, a good man; not no rich man, a good man;

one who works hard, plays hard, and knows how to have fun, who can love me in da midnight hour, till the mo-ning sun. I's looking for a good man, ya hear, not no handsome man, but a good man; not no tall man, but a good man, not no rich but a good man; one who . . ."

"Ms. Minnie!" Aunt Cellie screeched out.

Miss Minnie, mouth still open, stopped talking and looked at Aunt Cellie in shock.

Aunt Cellie said quickly, "Mr. Johnson's looking for a good woman, why don't ya—"

"Child, I done told ya: I don't want dat old toothless man! Why, one wrestle wit him and he be dead in t'ree mont's." She started down the hill, still talking to herself and anybody else: "I's be looking for a good man; not no handsome man, but a good man; not no tall man, a good man; not no rich man, a good man . . ." She turned and said, "If ya know where he be, tell him to come an see me. I's need me a good man!"

"Don't we all," said Aunt Cellie softly, bent over in her chair, with her elbows on her knees, snapping a bean ever so slowly. "I sho' could use a good man myself. There just ain't none left. After Ben died, I just give up 'cause there ain't nobody to take his place. I git lonesome, Lawd knows I do, but da Lawd is good. *He* my husband now."

"He said he would be," Ms. Noon said as she began to preach. "He said he would be a mother an a father, and I knows, I knows dat to be true, 'cause he been my mother an my father."

"Tell the truth!" shouted Ms. Nellie

"She just lonesome like me," said Aunt Cellie.

"Yeah, child," said Ms. Nellie, "I feel for ya, 'cause it ain't nothing like having a man around."

"Just keep on praying honey-child, keep on praying. Da good Lawd knows what ya need."

They kept on snapping beans quietly . . . .

For once, Ms. Nellie didn't have no gossip. Thea-Thea said she was like the local newspaper, knew everything on everybody and shared it. Thea-Thea would just shake her head, and say, "Well,

Nellie, what's new?" 'cause she knew, whether she wanted to hear it or not, Ms. Nellie was sure gonna tell it. Not today; her conversation was so sensible and quite touching as she talked about how she wanted to see if she could get the church to hold a *special prayer meeting* for Mr. Ed, Ms. Viv, Ms. Minnie, and the husband and wife that was murdered. "And Lawd, 'specially dem chilluns. No mama an no daddy, uhm, uhm, uhm."

"Ya know what, Nellie, dat's mighty sweet of ya. I thank it'll be a welcome request," said Thea-Thea.

Chapter Thirty-Four

Time Marches On

Well, time has passed and I've passed to the eighth grade, and doing quite well. Junior was going into the eleventh grade. They have closed down the little one-room schoolhouse I first attended, and the children were all now in what was the middle school.

Junior was captain of the football team. We were so proud of him. He really changed that boy, and playing him some ball, you hear me. He was the running back on the football team, and making touchdowns every game.

You talk about black people at these games, HUH, it was the highlight of the black community. The white kids had they own league. Only blacks played against blacks, and rivalry was high.

The bands were kicking, each one trying to out do the other. The band, cheerleaders, and fans from the other team on one side of the field, and the home team on the other side battling it out.

The cheerleaders in their little outfits... *man*, could they do their thing. They would clap and slap their hands and knees, hollering, *"BE AGGRESSIVE! BE AGGRESSIVE! B-E-A-GG-R-E-SS-I-V-E!!."* Ahhh, they had it down pat.

I told Thea-Thea excitedly, "That's what I am going to do when I get to the big school."

She said, "Honey Child, ya can be anythang ya want to be if ya keep gitting good grades."

"Yes, ma'am," I said as I repeated the cheer along with the girls and tried to do the dance.

The football team was known for beating just about every team they came in contact with, and that evening was no exception. They beat the other team like nobody's business.

At halftime, I saw this girl who had her eyes on my Junior, and I had my eyes on her. I gave her the "I'm watching you" gesture with my fingers to my eyes and pointing them back at her. *I think she got the message.*

The black football home games were always on a Saturday, during the day. The black schools didn't have a field to play on, so they used the white school fields. They were not allowed to use the locker rooms though, so they just stayed on the sidelines and rested. Some of them even played in the band at halftime. Now you talking 'bout a show, this was a showdown. The band was rocking, and the crowd was on their feet right with them, hollering "Git it, child! Git it..."

The majorettes would whirl and twirl and whip them skirts like nothing I'd ever seen. They were a beautiful sight. Their legs were every shade of browns and yellows, blending perfectly with the school colors of green and white.

The opposing band and cheerleaders would try to out-do ours, but honey, you had to have a bandleader and cheer coach like we had to do that. You could try all you wanted to...

These games were the highlight of my daddy's life. He was so proud of Junior. No matter what, he was not gonna miss a game.

The band struck out with, "I FEEL GOOD, DA-DA-DA-DA-DA."

"Uh-oh," Thea-Thea said, "I hope Ms. Nibby don't... *oh God!*" she screeched, "she's up there almost riding da mule!"

Ms. Nibby always had a ball. She was the highlight of the audience in the stands; everybody was clapping and cheering her on. She loved every minute of it. She didn't quite ride the mule, but she came real close.

Everybody was on their feet to the music. And we won the championship again, no surprise.

The coach was phenomenal, and he didn't *play*. Junior said, "he's 100 percent business."

My daddy really liked him, 'cause he kept the boys in line and on a very short leash. I even heard that he would hunt them down if he thought any of them were out partying during the season.

"Thea-Thea, I so wish Ludie could see this," I said sadly.

"Yes I know, baby, but she's so sick, and getting sicker all da time." Shaking her head, she said softly, "umh, umh, umh."

Russell came home from the army on short leave. My, he was sooooo handsome. All the women, old and young, in every camp were looking at my brother. He was tall and lanky, and looking *gooooood* in that army uniform. He had a rank too: PRIVATE FIRST CLASS. He said he thought he might stay in the service and make a career out of it.

He was already working on getting his GED. That boy was serious about his future. He had his fun while he was home, but took nothing with him when he left but memories.

He went to one of Junior's games while he was on leave in his uniform, and the girls were dropping like flies. You would have thought he was *James Brown* or somebody. Some of the guys were interested in what he had to say about the army. He was feeling really good when he had to return. He said that he felt he had made a positive impression on some of the young men.

I was really getting excited and eager to learn so that when I went to the "BIG" school, I was gonna be a force to be reckoned with.

The winter passed without incident except for the exciting times we had at the holidays.

Chapter Thirty-Five

TRAGEDY

"Oh *GOD!*" Thea-Thea screamed as the loud whistle blew. She ran to the front porch, and all of the other women were running out of their doors.

I had been packing to go to Virginia. Down the hill we went. Junior passed us running, hollering "What's happened?!"

"Oh God, DADDY!" he screamed.

The whistle never blew in the middle of the day unless it meant that something had happened at the mines. I had only heard it once in my lifetime and that was a trial test. But today, it was extra long and over and over. Something had happened. I was praying that one of our men had not been hurt, or even worse, killed.

We waited and waited. Cars were racing up the road to the mines.

"OH GOD!" someone yelled. "Somebody's done got killed!"

Mr. Man and the other men in the camp that was on the evening shift ran for the hill to the mines.

People from up the hollow were running down, and the people from the camp below were running up the road.

No one came to tell us anything, so we waited and waited, and worried. The women made coffee and brought it out to the people. The people, both black and white, were talking among themselves.

After what seemed forever, Mr. Man and the other men finally came down the hill, walking and talking and shaking their heads. By now, cars from other nearby communities were coming up the hollow. Every one gathered at the Crow Pole. We knew something bad had happened, and everyone was hollering for them to hurry and tell us something. But they stopped at the foot of the hill talking among themselves and didn't come any further.

Two ambulances were coming up the hollow, sirens blasting.

"Oh God, what has *happened* NAPO?" screamed Big Sis, calling Mr. Man's name and holding the baby in her arms as the other children held on to her legs crying, because everyone else was by now. I went over and gathered them up and took them inside the house to calm them down, giving them something to drink and cookies.

Little June said, "Bee-Bee, lets go back," pulling on my shirt.

"Okay, little buddy," I said, "okay, but we have to stay on the porch okay?"

"Okay," those who understood said. So back outside we went.

Thea-Thea was praying silently, walking and wringing her hands. I was crying and praying, "Lord don't let nothing happen to my daddy and big brothers, and *all* the others. Thank you Amen."

It seemed as if it took forever to get any news. Finally, the shift boss came down the hill, walking very slowly. Mr. Man and the rest of the men joined him as they walked toward the crowd. By now, white women and black women were embracing each other. The unknown was stifling. The shift boss walked up with his head down and took off his mining hat. He looked up and asked if any family members of Mr. John Kirby and Mr. Milton Spokes were there.

Everyone looked around and finally one of the white women said, "Noooo!" very mournfully and asked him a tearful, "*W*$_{HY}$?"

The shift boss cleared his throat and said, "They are buried under rock, and we fear that . . . that we may have lost them. We are going in to try to get to them, but . . . well, so . . . well, just pray for the safety of the men that are going in and for the souls of our two brothers—that's all."

He started throwing out orders for the men to prepare for the evening shift and assist the men on the day shift.

"Thea-Thea," I cried. "Where's Daddy, Oscar, and Frank?"

"Honey, they all right. They not da men that's trapped. They have to stay an help find da men . . . we just have ta pray . . . OH, THANK YA, LAWD . . . THANK YA!" she screamed.

All the women were now gathering around wondering which women were the widows, as all of them were crying hysterically. Finally, someone said, "They at work. They work down town in the five and ten-cent store."

"Oh GOD! Thea-Thea screamed, when she realized who was dead. Where's Sally's kids?!"

Some of the women took off down the road. Thea-Thea was weak from worry. She went to Big Sis's and sat on the porch rocking back and forth, praying and moaning. The babies all gathered around her wanting some Grandma loving, the baby trying to climb up in her lap. She reaches down through her tears and hugs them all.

Mary Jane, who lived up the hollow, was a newlywed of two years and had no children. She was so jolly and full of fun. Their little house was located on a hill just before you came to the next black camp up the hollow, friendly beyond words. She was very young and still a child at heart, so she was always inviting us girls in when we passed by to chat and eat snacks, and John was sooooo handsome. They were so in love. They reminded us of movie stars. She was so small and beautiful, with long brown hair. He would pick her up and toss her on the bed and shower her with kisses in front of us as she giggled, saying "Stop, John, not in front of the girls!"

"Oh my goodness, what will she do? What will she do?" I didn't know the other lady, but I was so sorry for her and her children.

Our hearts were heavy for their families. The women groaned in pain, crying with relief and sorrow. They got together on Big Sis's porch, discussing what to do when the women got home, which ones would go where so as to be of comfort to their "white sisters." They wanted to be there for them when the bodies were brought out. Solidarity was high; two of our own was GONE!

It was three days before miners' vacation. No one was in the mood now for the celebration that time of the year usually brought. We had some grieving to do.

Mr. Man and the other men got dressed in their bankers to go and help retrieve the bodies. The children went in their houses as some of the women went to the widows' houses.

Even though we were of two different worlds, when you're a coal miner, you're family. They wanted to be with the wives and children, so they would have as much support possible when the ambulances came by.

Someone had already gone to town to get the women whose loved ones were dead.

"OH GOD, OH GOD!" Thea-Thea wailed as we walked up the hill. She was holding on to Junior for support, weak from worry. She prayed all the way up the hill, thanking God for sparing her husband and her children. Then she got angry talking mostly to herself, "This is it! This is it! Cal is coming out of dat hole, and I mean it! Them boys gonna have to leave here and git out of dat mines! LAWD HAVE MERCY, LAWD HAVE MERCY," she cried.

I went to Big Sis's and helped her bring the children up the hill to the house. She and Thea-Thea sat on the porch and cried and cried.

When my daddy came home that night, I hugged him and cried, "Daddy, I want you to come out of that old mine."

He said, "don't worry, Princess, I be careful. I gota while to go 'fore I can re-tie, but soon enough, I will."

Thea-Thea said sternly, "Well, we gonna be looking into how much longer ya got to go, 'cause I ain't gonna lose ya and my babies to no hole in da ground, and then put ya in another one. No sirree!"

"I know, HoneyBabe," he said. "I sho is glad Russell didn't stay here and Junior ain't goin' in thar. I got two boys in thar, and dat's enough, dat's enough," he said, his shoulders slumped as he went in the house to change clothes.

He didn't have much of an appetite that night. He and Thea-Thea talked into the wee hours.

Me and Junior, overheard Daddy tell Thea-Thea, "Them men didn't have to die. They had done told da boss dat section was a time bomb, but nobody listened."

"Oh, Cal," Thea-Thea said, "Please, please be careful. Talk to da boys and try to convince 'em to go git a job somewhere else—Detroit maybe. I hear they got good jobs up there. I worry so much bout y'all."

"I know, HoneyBabe, I know," he said.

There was no work for days, as the BIG-WIGS came in to inspect. Well, it's a little too late . . . .

It was such a sad time. The ladies in all of the communities cooked and carried food and stuff to the widows. There was no denying the common bond that was felt by everyone. Sarah and I went to Mary Jane's house often to keep her company.

She was all alone now and very lonesome. She had packed a lot of her things in boxes. She said she was going to move back with her parents.

We cried, "We'll miss you so much!"

"I know, she said. "You girls been a great comfort to me, but I can't stay another day in this house; it holds too many memories. My parents on their way to load me up. I'm leaving today."

We cried and cried as we helped her fill up boxes and things. Soon, her parents and some other men were coming up the hill with a truck to move her away. She introduced us as her very best friends. Her mother hugged us and told us how glad she was that we were there for her Mary Jane.

"Yes, ma'am," we said, and then we left.

I was glad school was about to start back. It would be something to occupy my mind. This tragedy had really taken its toll on everyone . . . .

Chapter Thirty-Six

SPOILED?

Ludie had been feeling real poorly lately. She rarely came out on the porch anymore. I went to visit her every day. She was staying in bed most of the time now.

Ms. Francine said, "ClaraBy, you know Ludie is very sick and gitting sicker ever' day, so you got to be a big girl.... Okay?"

"Yes, ma'am," I said. I was trying hard not to cry, but my heart was breaking. Too much was happening at one time. I went into Ludie's room. She looked so tiny in the big bed. I knelt down on my knees and said the prayer that Ludie had taught me over time, the "Lord's Prayer." Then I said my bedtime prayer that I prayed each night. "Now I lay me down to sleep, I pray the Lord my soul to keep; if I should die before I wake, I pray the Lord my soul to take. God bless Thea-Thea, Daddy, Russell, Junior, Big Sis and her family, Oscar, and Frank ... and ... and *Lord, please, please* bless Ludie and me, AMEN. Oh, and LORD, please bless the family that lost their daddy and especially Mary Jane ... Amen ... again."

* * *

"Hey, Thea-Thea, Ms. Nellie said as she came up the steps. Thea-Thea was sitting on the porch. "Hey, Sweetie," she said as she greeted me, playing jack-rocks on the porch."

"How are you, Ms. Nellie?" I said as I went into the house. I made noise as if I were running up the steps. I stuck my head around the corner of the bottom step and peeped to see if all was clear for me to take my spot. It was.

"Honey-child," she started off, "have ya heard 'bout Tinys' girl?"

"No!" said Thea-Thea, anxious as to whether there was something bad wrong with her.

My ears perked up then.

Ms. Nellie said, "Child, she be knocked up."

"What?!" screeched Thea-Thea, "Which one?"

"Da baby girl, said Ms. Nellie. Yeah, child, ya know ya don't see her at church none lately. Ya know she . . . ."

Thea-Thea cut her off at that point. "Now, Nellie, let's just drop dat subject right here and now, 'cause ya know I don't talk bout nobody's chilluns. She's just a baby herself, only a year or two older than my ClaraBy, so I ain't gonna go there wit you, 'cause Lawd knows if dat fate ever befalls my baby, y'all be talking 'bout her too, and den ya know how dat's gonna turn out . . . ."

"Shit, Thea-Thea, ya ain't no fun. But ya right, I's got chilluns myself, and I feel da same way."

I had noticed that Janice had stopped coming to school. I'd asked Caroline where she was, and she said that she was feeling poorly. So one evening after school, I asked Thea-Thea if I could run up the hollow and see *Janice,* "'Cause Caroline says she's sick . . . ."

Thea-Thea turned around from the stove slowly and said, "ClaraBy, I can't allow ya to visit Janice, ya see she's done been spoiled."

"*Spoiled?*" I shouted while champing on a cold biscuit. "She smells all right to me; what did she eat?"

"Oh, ClaraBy," Thea-Thea said, "we gonna to have to have a talk, but not today, maybe tomorrow. Ya see Janice . . . done . . . something dat she shouldna . . . and it has spoiled her . . . and well . . . nice girls should stay away from her."

I could tell Thea-Thea was having a hard time explaining it to me. She was stuttering and stammering for words to say—like

"She's a nice girl, it's just dat well, she . . . oh heck, child, ya just can't go, dat's all! We'll talk bout it later."

Well, I was a little confused, 'cause I wasn't that hip about the birds and bees, just bits and pieces I had heard from the so-called *fast girls* at school. You did not want that label "fast." It seemed as if you couldn't even walk a certain way 'cause it made you *fast.*

Well, I was on my way, 'cause I was bow-legged you know, and you know what that means . . . . My Aunt Cellie used to say, "Honey Child, I'm little, but I'm loud; PO' . . . but I'm proud; bow-legged an know it—and I got da shape to show it." Heee, heee, heeeee!

She was bow-legged and big hipped and very pretty, and some of the other women couldn't stand that *"bitch,"* as I'd overheard two of the camp gossipers say while deep in conversation about the camp women they couldn't stand, while I was playing in the yard with Pearlie. They were sitting on Ms. Spencer's porch gossiping. They were from up the hollow. I think it was all because their men were on the wild side and they were on the *fat-ass side. Heeeee, Heeeee, Heeeeeeee!*

Never The Same

I have to say that this was the worst summer ever; it seemed as if everybody's lives had changed. The mining accident that killed those men had really dampened the spirits of all of the camps.

The men's conversation at the Crow Pole had changed. Now all they talked about was the accident, what should have happened, and what should not have happened. It was really a cruel wake-up call for them. It seemed to make everybody appreciate life more.

Daddy and the rest of the men were strong union men, and they were standing together to make sure that the families got their just due. You didn't mess with another union man, I don't care who you were.

Often during the summer, Daddy and the men would strike, and when one mine struck, all miners struck. It was a domino effect. The union halls would be full every Saturday with retired miners as well, discussing the woes of the conditions in the mines and what they were going to do about them.

When a strike was imminent, Daddy said every man in every mine, when the word got around, would pour their water out of their buckets and turn around and come back home. It meant no pay, but it sure meant self respect and unity. They didn't play about crossing the picket line. Cross if you dare, and end up with a bashed-in head, or worse . . . .

Mr. Man, my sister, and the kids would come up to the house, and we'd all sit on the porch and listen to them talk about what was going on at the mines. Sometimes they might let it slip that the mines were unsafe. Then they would have to back-track and rephrase what they had said, 'cause my sister and Thea-Thea would be getting upset.

Daddy would say something like "No, no, HoneyBabe, I don't mean *unsafe,* unsafe, I mean unsafe when ya careless, or somethin' like dat." Then they would change the subject.

During the hard times was when the community pooled their resources and shared everything with each other. Nobody went hungry even if it was beans every day. *Nobody* went hungry.

THE *P* WORD

Now on Saturday mornings, the Crow Pole was full of men who came from down the road or other communities, who worked in other mines, would often speak about the conditions in their mines and would be getting *rawled* up about how some of the men were being treated.

"The black man gota hard way da go. They knowed I could handle dat dang machine better than Henry; they just didn't want to give dat job to no black man. Henry didn't have to lose his leg if he'd listened to me. 'Noooo,' Mr. Jones said, with a little smirk on his face. Serves they asses' right.

"I sho' hope Henry gits justice for his leg; he's gota lota mouths to feed. I hate to say it, but it serves 'em right. They got-ta pay a big fine for unsafe working conditions, but dat don't help Henry none. What he gon' do now?"

Mr. Simpson said chewing on a piece of birch wood, "What he gon' do? The union gat-ta steps in and help da boy, 'cause he sho' gonna need it wit all them chilluns."

Stories like these went on all the time anymore. It seems as if a dark cloud had descended over all the communities. It was hard getting over the tragedy, and it had seemed to trigger other issues that were not often talked about—the big P word. Prejudice! I really didn't know what they were talking about, but they were fired up about it.

The worst summer ever, I tell you.

Chapter Thirty-Seven

PRAISE THE LORD... I THINK

The one good thing was, Daddy had started going to *church*.

"HALLELUJAH!" Thea-Thea shouted as he came up from the back to give the pastor his hand. Ms. Lula, Ms. Minnie, and Ms. Maxwell were shouting all over the place, turning over benches and things.

I loved when the *Holy Spirit*, as they called it, came to church. Everybody got *ugly* praising the Lord. The pastor, Reverend Berry, was screaming something and pounding on the podium. The women in the choir were falling backward and carrying on. I had never seen it like this in all my years. Thea-Thea was in her own little world over in the corner behind the coal stove, shouting up a storm. Several women were fanning her like crazy, but letting her have her way.

Ms. Margaret, who was sitting on the front seat across from the choir stand and the deacons' bench, got up and started *shouting*. She shouted all the way over to the other side and fell in Deacon Smith's arms.

Well, all *hell* broke loose, 'cause Sister Smith leaped out of the choir stand and grabbed Ms. Margaret! I thought she was assisting her, until I saw that she had her hands around her throat, squeezing! Deacon Smith was trying to pry her hands apart. She let go of her throat with one hand and started pulling her hair with the other hand. She was squeezing hard and pulling hard!

Reverend Berry was hollering from the podium, trying to get the crowd quiet, but nobody was listening anymore. Everybody was either involved in trying to see the fight—or should I say the beat-down—or crying and calling on the *Lord* to please intervene.

Finally, Ms. Smith let go of Ms. Margaret and turned and socked Deacon Smith so hard that his glasses went three rows back! She stood straight up, smoothed out her dress, and then turned to walk out. The people in her path parted like the Red Sea.

Hee, Heeeee, Honey, it was quite a sight! I didn't quite know what was going on, but I didn't have to wonder long. Soon as the children were fed and sent out to play, the "camp gossipers" came to sit on our porch late that evening after everything had quieted down. I had finished my chores, but I was upstairs in my room gathering my dolls to take to Ludie's for my playtime, so I went unnoticed for the time being.

"Here they come," Daddy told Thea-Thea as he got up to go in the house and out the backdoor to sit on the back porch or wherever.

"Oh Lawd," Thea-Thea said, "I'm really gonna enjoy this session. Heeee heeee, I thought Sylvia was praising da Lawd, I didn't know what was going on I was so high in da spirit."

"I know, HoneyBabe," Daddy replied, "it just made me realize dat church ain't gonna git ya inta heaven. I coulda stayed out here and saw dat.... I have to say though, it was quite a sight. I wouldna missed it for da world!"

"Yeah, but ya needed to be fed da word, so don't have no regrets; da angel's shouting."

"Sho' ya right, HoneyBabe," he said. "Ladies," he said as he tipped his head as if he had a hat on, and he headed for the door.

"Cal!" yelled Ms. Nellie. "I's sho' proud of ya, *proud,* I tell ya."

"Yessir," said the other women as they hit the steps.

Daddy said, "Thank ya kindly," as he made his escape.

Thea-Thea, Big Sis, and Aunt Cellie were already on the porch and were joined by Ms. Nellie, Ms. Nibby, Ms. Francine. One by one they grabbed a seat, laughing, getting ready for the gossip session.

Ms. Nellie was the last one to come up the steps, and she came talking. "Heeee, heeeeee, Lawd, Lawd, I ain't never seen nobody move as fast as Sylvia today. Hee, heeeeeeee." She slapped her leg. "Everybody knows Margaret's done been going wit Deacon Smith! I don't know why Sylvia ain't whooped her ass 'fore now."

"Yeah," Ms. Nibby said, "she *bold* wit her stuff, ya know. I don't know what Frank sees in dat gal. She's been nothin' but bad news ever since she hit town," she continued.

Big Sis spoke up and said, "Well, I'll tell you what, I've been laying back, not saying much, but I heard that she had her eyes on Napo . . . . Now, you ain't seen no ass-whooping as I'm gonna put on her if I hear one more *thang*. Oh, 'scuse me, Thea-Thea, I mean butt-whooping."

"Oh, dat's okay, child, ya grown now, and if ya thank some *strag* after yo man, I'm all for ya whooping dat butt."

Everybody fell out laughing.

"But," Thea-Thea continued as she got dead serious and leaned toward her first daughter, "remember this and remember it well, Big Sis: It takes two to tango. Don't give yo man no pass, 'cause where there's smoke there's fire, and da man is usually holding da match—just remember dat."

"Ain't dat da truth," said Ms. Nellie, "a man is just a dog in a pair pants."

They all agreed. But I was puzzled, 'cause I *knew* my daddy was no dog! No sirree, not my daddy.

The conversation got deeper and deeper as they raked Ms. Margaret over the coals.

"Uh-oh, speaking of dogs," Ms. Nellie said, "here comes one who thanks he's a pit bull tipping out for his regular Sunday evening getaway."

It was Mr. Penn taking his usual Sunday evening stroll. He was a very frail-looking man, and his wife was always beating him up. He worked on the same shift as my daddy.

"I'm 'fraid one of these days Ethel gonna kill him," Thea-Thea said.

"Yes, Lawd," Ms. Nibby said. "She done darn near did it a couple of times, but it don't do no good; he right back to his old tricks."

Mr. Penn said, "Good evening, ladies! Fine evening, ain't it."

They all said, "Sho' nuff is Penn."

"How's Ethel doing? We missed her at church today," said Ms. Nellie.

"Oh," he said, "She feeling a little poorly, but she be fine—yes, sir, she be fine. Well," he said, fidgeting around from foot to foot. "I best be on my way, uhh . . . da doctor told me to walk and I tries to follow da doctor's orders, ya know . . . bad heart an all . . . Y'all have a good day now," he said, tipping his hat as he went over the hill toward the church, heading up the hollow.

"Bad heart, my big toe, he got a bad heart all right, and it ain't in his chest," said Ms. Nibby. They all fell out laughing.

"Umh, umh, umh, 'doctor,' my beeee-hind, he must thank we just got off da turnip truck. Bea sho' must have what he needs, 'cause he don't care how many ass-whoopings he git, he goes right back up dat hollow," said Ms. Nibby, shaking her head.

"Well, ya know, two of dem kids is his," said Ms. Francine. "She had 'em *waaay* after she came here, wit no *husss* . . . band. She claims he died; truth be tol', she never had no man of her own."

"Well," Ms. Nellie said, "I hear he's packing a load in them britches."

They all screamed with laughter.

"Dat'll do it ever time!" Ms. Nellie squealed.

"WHAT?" After that, I started watching Mr. Penn to see what he was packing in his britches, 'cause he was so frail, I was afraid it was too heavy for him. After all, I was just a kid and not very hip, so forgive me for being a little naïve.

Oh, I failed to tell you: Ms. Margaret is my oldest brother Frank's wife—well, his ole lady, common-law wife, whatever. She came to town some years ago during miners' vacation with some friends of Ms. Nellie's from over on the "W," (a coal county about 40 miles away.) found her a sucker (my brother), and never left. She thinks she's all that and a bag of chips—do I have to say what I think she's a bag of? Yeah, you got it . . . She wasn't a bad-looking girl, just had a missing tooth in the front.

True to Her Word

Well, lo and behold, a week almost to the day, such a commotion was going on down the hill. People had gathered on this beautiful sunshiny day, and somebody was getting a butt-whooping.

"THEA, THEA!"

Ms. Francine was hollering, "Come quick, Evelyn is gitting it on wit Margaret!"

"OH LAWD!" screeched Thea-Thea as she ran wildly off the porch and down the hill. Daddy just sat on the porch rocking, telling Thea-Thea to be careful and don't fall.

The boys' basketball game came to a screeching halt as they bolted up the road to see the excitement.

Well, I knew not to go running as I wasn't authorized to go play as yet. The kids were on the porch crying and Daddy said, "Baby Girl, go tend dem younguns."

"Yes sir!" I screamed as I ran as fast as my little legs would go.

Now, when Thea-Thea got to the fight, Mr. Man was trying to separate them by trying to pull Big Sis off of Margaret. Well, Thea-Thea went upside his head with a right hook, 'cause he was letting Margaret get a hold of my sister's blouse and tearing it off. He backed up real quick as Thea-Thea put her foot on Margaret's chest and gave my sister a shove. I believe Thea-Thea may have mashed her foot down a little hard, but Margaret was grateful for the relief.

Ms. Margaret scrambled to get up. Thea-Thea said loudly, "WHAT DA HELL Y'ALL STANDING ROUND FOR?" They scattered like sheep. It was the first time I had seen my Thea-Thea mad . . . and cussing too! She was hot as a pot-bellied stove that had just been stoked . . . Heeee, Heeee!

Mr. Man went in the house behind Big Sis like a little puppy trying to explain.

Thea-Thea shouted at Margaret, "WHERE FRANK?"

Margaret said quietly, "He at home."

Thea-Thea spat out, "Dat's where yo ass oughta be!"

Ms. Margaret started picking up the groceries until she heard Big Sis coming back out the door. She started running up the hollow as fast as she could.

Heee, heeeee, Big Sis had come out the door for some more whoop-ass, while Mr. Man was trying to hold her back.

Big Sis was telling him to "Turn me loose, I'm gonna deal with you in a minute! But I ain't finished with this bitch yet."

Thea-Thea turned and told her son-in-law to "Turn her loose, and I mean *turn her loose!*"

Needless to say, he turned her loose. Thea-Thea got Big Sis by the arm and they went in the house to try to calm Big Sis down and get the skinny on what had happened. Well, by now, I was consoling the children who were crying, and so . . . I could hear everything that was said . . .

Big Sis began by saying, "I was sitting in the window looking down the road shelling beans, when I saw Margaret coming up the road with grocery bags in her arms. "Margaret couldn't see me behind the sheers at the window, and Napo thought I was in the kitchen. So I got up and went to the window facing the front porch and the road, standing behind the sheer curtain where I could see both of them.

"Napo was sitting in the corner of the porch with his feet propped upon the banister, reading the newspaper. I saw Margaret wink at Napo, and Napo smiled and winked back. Well, that was enough, it was ON."

Thea-Thea told Mr. Man sarcastically, "Well, I guess YOU had better not be so friendly da next time."

Mr. Man looked like that little stray dog as he tried to explain. "I . . . I . . ." he stuttered.

"'I . . . I . . .' WHAT . . . WHAT?!" screamed Big Sis.

Thea-Thea turned to Big Sis and said, "Ya know you don't discuss yo business in front of da chilluns . . . . BUT . . . *HANDLE YO BUSINESS*!" And she took me by the arm, turned and said, "Remember *da match*," and she made a gesture as if she was blowing a match out.

We went up the hill at high speed, I could hardly keep up with her. She was *red hot.*

Daddy had not moved a muscle; he was rocking back and forth with his pipe as if nothing had happened. Thea-Thea plopped down in her rocking chair and began to fill him in . . . . I went in the house . . . as I knew I should . . . .

Chapter Thirty-Eight

OH BROTHER

Man, my brothers sure know how to pick 'em. Late, late one night, BANG, BANG, BANG on the back door. When Daddy got to the door, my second oldest brother was standing there in his *tighty-whities*, barefooted as a river duck, out of breath. He had come across the church hill in the dark of night, running for his life. He fell in the door.

Daddy noticed that he was bleeding from his head and arm. "What happened?" Daddy asked.

"She cut me," Oscar said. "She crazy!" he said, "crazy, I tell ya!"

Thea-Thea got up and went in the kitchen to see what was wrong. Me and junior were in our usual position, trying to listen through the vent in his room over the kitchen.

Oscar said that Mamie (his ole lady, common-law wife, whatever) and him had been drinking and having a little party, just the two of 'em. He accidentally called her by his other old lady's name, who he'd had before he met her, and all hell broke loose.

"Umh, umh, umh," Thea-Thea said, as she attended his arm. "I don't know why you and Frank don't just leave them crazy Alabama sleazies alone.... Ya work hard every day, and it seems like ya can't please her. She spends every dime ya make, fixing dat raggedy-butt house up till it looks like a *mausoleum*, and she still ain't satisfied. This makes da third time she done sent ya home wounded! ... What you gon' do—let her kill ya!?"

Daddy said harshly, "I's about had it wit' her, son. Now ya gonna have ta do somethin'."

"Yeah, I know," Oscar said, looking very sad. "I've had enough this time."

Mamie had moved here with her aunt and uncle the Simmons, and was kind of *on the rough side.* She was always bullying somebody. Word was that she came here on the run for stabbing somebody. She thought she was a *bad mamma-jamma.*

Well, Oscar was true to his word. Mamie went to town with Margaret the next Saturday morning, and when she got back home, Oscar had packed all his things and every thing else he could into his car and left town. He didn't even tell Thea-Thea and Daddy he was leaving; he just did.

Mamie came down to the house after she discovered that he was gone, demanding to know where he was.

Daddy told her that he didn't know that he was gone, and that maybe he was just down the road.

She was raging, she said, "Ya know damn well he gone and where he gone!"

Thea-Thea came out on the porch, wiping her hands on her apron and asked, "What's da matter?"

Daddy said, "Mamie say looks like Oscar gon' and left."

"*Left?*" Thea-Thea screamed, "what ya mean *left?*"

Mamie huffed herself all up like she was going to challenge Thea-Thea, shaking her finger at Thea-Thea. "Ya know damn well what I mean, and ya know where he at. So don't give me dat *I don't know* bullshit."

Daddy rose up and said, "Now . . . I ain't Oscar, and ya won't bring yo sorry ass to my porch and demand dat we tell you *nothin.* Yo'd better git the hell away from here 'fore ya can't . . . . Another thang: don't ya ever raise yo voice at HoneyBabe. Don't I'll whoop yo ass myself."

Thea-Thea said, "Oh, don't ya worry none, Cal; she don't want none of me. I'll sift her like bread flour and pour her butt down da toilet. Now, git yo foot off my step 'fore I make a step." Thea-Thea started toward the steps.

Mamie turned like she was told and started walking off, cursing every breath.

I was upstairs listening out of the window, boxing the air and talking to myself, 'cause I wanted a piece of her too.

Oscar wrote Thea-Thea after a few weeks and told her he was all right. He was in Missouri and was working in a factory, making pretty good money. Thea-Thea was so happy.

She said, "Thank Ya, Lawd, my child is safe, I can sleep now."

Well, I thought, *one down and one to go . . . .*

Chapter Thirty-Nine

WHOOPEE!

Thank God school is starting—maybe things will get back to normal. I've passed to the ninth grade, and I'm on my way to that high school . . . way down the road.

I had not seen Janice all summer. She had not come out of the house, nor out of the hollow. I dared not ask—as I was not to mention her name at all. So I didn't have her to show me around on my first day at the big school.

I was scared to death. I didn't know what to do or where to go when we arrived. It looked like the big scary house I had seen in the *Archie* funny books at Halloween time.

Junior was sitting in the back of the bus with the bigger kids, laughing and talking, not paying me any attention. My stomach was in knots. I was not alone; some of the other kids who were going for their first time were just as scared as I was.

Thea-Thea had told him to watch out for me, but noooo, he was busy jive-talking with the bigger kids in the back of the bus.

As we began to get off the bus, he hollowed for me to wait for him. "*Whooo,* I thought, thank God he remembered he had a little sister to take care of.

He got off the bus and took me by the hand. He saw how nervous I was. He said, "Don't worry, Baby Girl, you'll be all right. It's not that bad."

There was a man standing at the big double doors, welcoming the kids back to school. Some he called by name. When Junior and I reached him, he said, "Hello, Calvin" (which is Junior's real name, as he is named after Daddy), "welcome back." Then he said, "Who have we here?"

Junior said, "This is my sister, ClaraBy, Mr. Stevens, it's her first year."

Mr. Stevens said, "Welcome to Bulldog High, ClaraBy."

"Thank you," I replied softly, scared to death.

Junior said, "That's the principal, Baby Girl," as we went through the doors. "He's the boss."

Well, I felt better just knowing that my big brother was in the building. He took me straight to the principal's office, where he helped get my assigned room. Then he was off to his room, hollering, "I'll probably see you later. Just remember all the things I've told you over the summer!"

"Okay" I said, as he dashed off. *Well, here goes,* I thought as I entered the room, along with some of the other first-timers, and took my assigned seat.

Ms. Coles was my teacher. She was a tiny, soft-spoken woman.

I thought, *Okay, she's not going to be too tough.* Boy was I wrong—she ruled with an iron fist! The first thing she said, after she had introduced herself, welcomed us, and called the roll, was "ALL RIGHT, RULE NUMBER ONE: no talking, no chewing gum, no snickering . . . no, no, no."

I had never heard the word so much in all my days. I thought, *Oh Lord, what have I gotten myself into?* The whole class looked scared to death.

Well, I got through the hard part of getting used to the rules, and they weren't so hard to do, because the same rules had applied from my very first day in school, only Ms. Deskins hadn't said them quite so forcefully. I could tell in an instance that this little lady didn't play. So I got down to business, 'cause I knew Thea-Thea didn't play either.

As time would have it, I adjusted very well, as did the other first-timers. It seemed to me, though, that the bigger kids thought we weren't of any significance. They didn't include us in *anything*. It seemed that it was all about them: the sophomores seemed to cater to the juniors and seniors' every command. I don't even think that there was a name for us except the ninth graders. Oh yeah, *freshmen*.

It seemed as if we were second-class citizens in a world of snobs—we were the only class that could not leave the campus for lunch. *What a crock!* I thought.

We were told that there was a snack shop at the foot of the hill, and they went there to eat. We could see them running in bunches back to the school so they would beat the bell. Junior said you dared not miss being in class when that bell rang or you were in deep do-do.

The teachers were very strict with their rules and teaching. We caught on real quick, seeing the boys who missed the bell having to bend over in the hallway and receive the *bull-board*. Heeee-Heee-Heeee.

The girls had another form of punishment. They had to hold their hands out to get the whack—and were only allowed to be punished by a female teacher, which was usually Ms. Washington. *Whooooo!*

She was a big woman, every bit of six feet tall, with huge breasts and a heavy voice. She was a man wrapped up in a woman's body if I ever saw one. All of the girls were totally convinced of that, even though she was the mother of five kids. I am here to tell you. She did not play.

She wore her hair back in a bun, which made her look matronly—or sort of like a prison warden or something. When she had hall duty, she always had the paddle in her hand, and she would hit her palm with it as she gazed up and down the hall. Even the boys were totally scared of her. I just knew that I never wanted to face her in my life time, no sirreeeee!

School was very exciting and new. We had *sock hops*. Now you talking about a good time! I would dance my little legs off with Olive and Pearlie. Don't worry, I didn't ride the mule—I sure didn't want that word attached to me: *fast*.

The girls and boys were allowed to dance together only on fast records—no slow records were ever played—so no boyfriend or girlfriend hugging went on at any time.

Football practice was going on, and the atmosphere was full of exciting anticipation. *Here's my big chance!* Cheerleading tryouts were about to begin. I had been practicing and practicing. I didn't have any decent shorts to wear for the tryouts, so I took my best pair of pajama pants and rolled them up as far as I could get them above my knees, so that they were tight against my legs.

I didn't make it. One of the legs of my PJs fell down, and off I ran in shame!

So, after the fact that it seemed as if no one had paid me any attention during the try outs, I escaped unscathed.

I dug into my books, vowing to try again next year, *with a real pair of shorts.* "Why didn't I cut the legs of the old pair of pajamas I had, why?" I asked myself that question a thousand times. "Oh well."

Football season has arrived! The first game was coming up, and the whole school was hyped up. The day before the game, the school had a *Pep Rally.* Man, you talking about exciting, I was in heaven.

Olive, Pearlie, me, and Carolyn always sat as close together as we could. Carolyn was in my homeroom and we had become friends, so she was now an official part of the pack.

Each homeroom came in one at a time. Everything was noisy but orderly until the team came in. The noise was deafening—everyone was screaming. Then the cheerleaders came in turning flips and doing back-handsprings. The football *boys* led the first cheer: "BULLDOGS, BULLDOGS, BULLDOGS!

The band was on the stage rocking out a special tune that really got us going. The cheerleaders were doing their special dance to the tune. We were ecstatic.

I tell you, Honey Child, those cheerleaders would be doing their thing, and the band was *hot.* The football boys would get up and give their famous yell: "RUFF-RUFF-RUFF," over and over. The whole gym would go up in a roar, "RUFF-RUFF-RUFF!" It was *game-on* then. They were out for blood.

The first year in the big school was exciting, to say the least—just being there among the big kids.

I had begun to "bud" quite rapidly. Thea-Thea said my body was taking shape—as was the other girls.

The boys seemed to be getting taller, and their voices were heavier. Some of them even had some hair on their lips. I was beginning to notice how cute some of them were.

Junior wasn't lying about the pretty girls. They were all around, but they had nothing on some of the girls in my grade—including me—except we were dumb as dirt to the facts of life.

I had already "come into womanhood," so I was somewhat prepared—Thea-Thea had told me all about it. But where babies came from I still was sort of dumb, because where I was told they came from I knew was impossible. There is no way.

Thea-Thea had tried to inform me by telling me when I *came into womanhood*, not to let no boy get on top of me, and then she said, "Well, I'll tell you more later."

Big Sis tried to tell me, but every time she started to talk, the kids would start fighting, or something would interrupt us. "Don't worry, I'll tell you later," she'd say.

Sooooo, one evening, I came home from school, and Thea-Thea told me that Janice had been visited by the *Big Bird* and had a baby boy.

Oooookaaayyy! Now I was totally confused. The kids never talked about Janice. It was as if she didn't exist.

Her sister never said anything about her, and we never asked. So it was quite a shock to know that she'd had a baby. "How? Why? What? What the world? What the world! The Big Bird theory again . . . *Yeah, right!*

I was dying to see her, but I knew I would not be allowed to. But one Saturday afternoon, I could stand it no longer, I swallowed my nerves and said, "Thea-Thea, can I go see Janice and the baby?"

She said, "Well, I guess it's okay. Ya coming of age now, and ya need to know some very necessary things. But only stay an hour ya hear? And don't ask no questions. We gonna have a woman-to-girl talk tonight okay?"

"Yes, ma'am!" I screamed as I ran down the steps heading up the hollow.

I wasn't even scared, because Mr. G-Baby was sitting on the Crow Pole telling lies with the other men. I ran across the church hill and came down the side of Ms. Maxwell's and Mr. G-Baby's shanties, past the cemetery, up the hollow I went as fast as my little legs would carry me.

I knocked on Janice's screen door. Mr. Simmons came to the door and saw it was me. He seemed shocked as he smiled and said, "Come on in, child." He seemed to be glad that someone was coming to visit.

He was a strange man; he never mingled with any of the other men. They kept to themselves pretty much, except for church. Even though they had been to church every Sunday without Janice, it was never discussed in any of the gossip sessions. He was the adult Sunday school teacher, and deeply religious. Daddy said, he was one of the finest men he knew.

They had kin people who visited very often—on both sides of the family—from Kentucky, and they often visited them, so they were never lonesome or anything.

Mrs. Simmons was a beautiful woman. She was quite heavy, with a very beautiful complexion that looked like toffee candy. Her dark brown hair was mingled with gray, and she kept it in a bun. She reminded me of my granny's sister. She smiled when she saw me and said, "Come on in, child. Janice's been expecting ya. Where have ya been?"

"Well," I said, "I ah, I just . . ."

"Oh, dat's okay, child, I understand," she said, leading me into the bedroom where Janice was.

Janice's eyes lit up when she saw me. I ran over to the bed and hugged her.

"I know why you ain't been up here, but don't worry about it. I know you would have if you could."

"What you got there?" I said.

Janice smiled real big and said, "He's a blessing, ClaraBy. No matter what nobody says."

I was amazed at this little guy. He was so sweet looking, sleeping and sucking his tongue. I thought, *That's how Paula looked after a week or two* . . . I just had to touch his face. He was as soft as cotton. Janice and I just stared at him. I didn't ask her no questions, as

Thea-Thea had told me that it was nobody's business. So I left it at that.

I filled her in on all of the latest at school, telling her how much I missed her not being there. She said that she was still going to study from her sister's books as much as she could, and that one of these days, she would finish her education, but right now, her life was only to raise her child.

I said, "Well, I'll come and visit as often as I can and keep you up on everything."

"Okay," she said.

I stayed as long as I thought I should. We hugged, and I gently patted that beautiful little baby boy as I said goodbye.

"ClaraBy?"

"Uh-huh," I replied.

"Thanks for coming," she said, with tears in her eyes.

I just smiled at her.

Running down the road, I began to think about that *big bird*. Why in the world had he brought Janice a baby? I kept looking up in the sky—so if I see it coming at me, I can kick the—oops, well, I was bound and determined that he wouldn't be leaving no baby for me. No sirreeeee!

Chapter Forty

Hog-Killing Time & Holidays

"Baby Girl, Baby Girl!," Daddy was calling me this chilly November Saturday morning. It was hog-killing time, and today they were going to slaughter two hogs for Mr. Cecil.

I woke up saying, "Sir."

"Come down here, Daddy needs to talk to ya," he said.

"Yes sir," I said as I swung my feet out of bed into my house shoes and ran downstairs. "Yes sir?" I said.

Rubbing his hands together he said, "Baby Girl, ya know its hog-killing time, and I'm gonna have to put Big Red down next week."

"(I had to rename her after she had gotten so big, so I had started calling her Big Red." Little girl I said, rubbing her back, you have grown so much I think I'm gonna have to start calling you "Big Red,") She was so beautiful. I had noticed that Daddy had put her in the special place that was no longer on the ground and she could only be fed corn, but you know me, DUH! I never bothered to ask why for once in my life.

"Oh no Daddy I cried, you can't kill Big Red! She, she, she's my pet!

"I know, Baby Girl, but ya knowed this day was gonna come sooner or later. I's just put it off and put it off, but now she done got too big, and we gonna need dat meat for da winter months, and . . ."

"*Meat?! Meat?!*" I cried, "Surely you're not gonna eat Big Red? No, Daddy, Nooooo!" I cried. "Ooooooh, Thea-Thea, please don't let them kill Big Red!"

Thea-Thea said, "Now listen, child, ya got to be brave about this. Every child done give up they pet pig but you. Ya got to let go now. There will be more piglets, an ya can start all over again, but know before ya choose one, dat one day it will be on da table."

I cried a little longer, and then I said, "Can I walk with her?"

Daddy and Thea-Thea looked at each other and shrugged their shoulders, and said, "We'll see, we'll see."

"Well, *I'm* not going to eat any of her. I just can't!"

"Okay," Thea-Thea said rolling her eyes around, "ya won't have to."

So the following Saturday morning, early, the camp was bustling again preparing for the BIG KILL. The women were busy making fires in the cook stoves and getting plenty of buckets and tubs for the meat.

Mr. Ed and the other men in the camp worked hard making a massive fire under the big long barrel they used to slide the hog down in the hot, hot water.

One by one, the hogs were brought to slaughter.

Mr. Ed was the Hog-Killing Master. He would gut the hogs and drink some of the blood—as an omen, I guess. It was quite a sight for us kids to see how he so skillfully did his work. I thought, *Poor Ms. Viv, I hope she never makes him mad enough to do her like he does the hogs.*

"ClaraBy! ClaraBy!," J. J. and Buster screamed, snapping me back to reality, "Here comes Big Red."

Mr. Ed and Daddy were escorting Big Red down the hill. She was beautiful, red as she could be. She was so fat, her belly was almost touching the ground. I had kinda gotten used to the idea that she was going to be sacrificed, and Ludie had helped me to understand the necessity of having food for the hard winter months and beyond. She had told me how they would take Big Red's fat and make soap for scrubbing, and how some would be given to the neighbors like Sarah and J. J.'s family, so that would have food. The hogs didn't seem to suffer very much before it was all over.

The men were busy at work bringing the guts in for the women to clean, as they were a delicacy. *Chitterlings*, a poor man's caviar.

Ms. Nellie's house was nearest the killing ground, and she was only too happy to have the meat butchered and cleaned there, because she was well-compensated. Thank God we had finally got running water in the houses!

The women would be busy, and the kitchen would be smelling good as the women would fry fresh tenderloin. Yum, yum, yum!

Thea-Thea was the master of pork skins. She would render the lard out of the skin in the oven and make it very crispy, salt it down, and give each child a hearty piece of crispy skin. Yum, yum, yum! Sorry Big Red. The lard fat was placed in containers for use later.

Every child would wait for the bladder, as we used it for a balloon. I got Big Red's.

Thanksgiving Day

Thanksgiving Day was a special time in the community. The women were busy during the week while the men were at work and children in school, getting ready for Thursday morning. Food galore was being prepared in each house to be carried to the church.

School was out, and the mines were closed for the holiday. It was going to be a good day.

Turkeys were being prepared, hams, yams, greens, green beans, corn, okra, stuffing, corn bread, rolls, macaroni and cheese, potato salad, macaroni salad, casseroles of any kind that you could think of.

Ms. Elsie Jackson fixed a delicious broccoli casserole. She could make a meal out of anything, just like my Thea-Thea. She lived down the road in another camp but came to our church every Sunday with Mr. Simpson.

She said, "Child, I can't deal wit dem folks down there in dat church, they all hypocrites. They done did ever-thang in da world, an now all holy an all. Can't stand hypocrites, ya hear, can't stand 'em. They don't half speak, nose all turned up in da air, fanning like they all hot an bothered. Ain't nothin but guilty conscience, guilty, ya hear. Da men old and wore out, can't hear, an da wives thank ya still want 'em. Guilty, I tell ya, *guilty*. Anytime a woman *don't* speak, she done had yo man, an now she scared ya got yo eye on hers, if she got one, an if they speak too sweet, ya bet she done had 'em. They just don't know me—I done had my fun if I don't git, well no more, Honey Child!" Heee, Heeeee.

The church was packed. People had long since got the word about Thanksgiving in Clear Water Hollow—even those who had prepared their meals at home came and brought a dish. It just seemed that no one wanted to be alone on this day.

There was so much food! Our white friends were always invited to come, and sure enough, some of them showed up every year, bringing their favorite dishes.

Pies and cakes sat on every windowsill.

Everyone seemed to be so grateful to God for his blessings. We were all so happy.

The men brought tables and placed them just below the pulpit in the front of the church. The women would get together to see what was on the menu and who was fixing what.

What food was left was given to the less fortunate like Mr. G-Baby, Ms. Maxwell, Ms. Minnie, and others, with specific orders not to eat it after a certain length of time, especially the potato salad and dressing.

My Thea-Thea did three turkeys. Child, you ain't tasted no turkey and dressing until you taste my mama's. The gravy was something indescribably delicious. "The recipe is a secret, an if I tol' ya, I'd have to do ya in," she would say, laughing heartily. Daddy liked a little oyster dressing, so she made a separate pan for him.

Every household that came had to bring plates and silverware to eat with, saucers for the kids, etc. It was so neatly organized. Buckets of water were pumped from the well in the front of the church and brought in and sat on a table, with a dipper in each one.

I was helping dress the tables when I heard laughing and bustling at the door. In came Mr. and Mrs. Simmons, Caroline, Janice, and the baby. I ran to her as she came in with her head held high. Everyone was gathering around her to see the little bundle of joy.

It was a sight to see the ole gossiping bags pretend that they hadn't talked about her like a dog, smiling and coochie-cooing the baby, trying to guess who he looked like.

Mrs. Simmons had baked pies and cakes, which Mr. Simmons gladly handed off to Aunt Cellie.

Janice and I went over by the choir stand where the younger ones were gathering. The kids were all curious and wide-eyed at the beautiful baby boy who was smiling up a storm at everyone. We were all so happy to see Janice, I didn't care if she had two heads and three arms. She was *my* friend!

Everybody was laughing and eating. We had a *feast*, I tell you. We ate and ate, and played and played on the church ground until almost dark.

It was so wonderful to see Mr. Monroe, Ms. AnnaBelle, Sarah, and J. J. enjoying the day. Yes, I said Mr. Monroe! He had straightened up a lot, Daddy said.

"He's done started doing what he shoulda been doing all da time. His health done played out now; he gotta stay home. Well, I guess dat's how it goes."

Ms. AnnaBelle sang "Bless this House, Oh Lord We Pray." The whole church was crying with Thanksgiving.

After the evening meal and the singing, Ms. AnnaBelle went up to Ms. Francine and gave her a big hug, as if she were making peace with her *and* God. Mr. Cecil just sat there stiff as a board, taking quick glances at Aunt Cellie, who was giving him a mean eye. He was scared to death of her still yet. His eyes were begging her not to give him away.

Aunt Cellie gave him that *I've-got-my-eyes-on-you* look. If there was such a thing as s*cared straight*, then Mr. Cecil was a poster child.

As soon as the weekend after Thanksgiving had passed, the whole camp was preparing for the next big holiday, the biggest one of all.

Chapter Forty-One

CHRISTMAS!

It seemed to be in the air. Neighbors were excited, telling each other who was coming home for the holidays.

School was so much fun this time of year. Our music teacher, Ms. Miller, was preparing a concert with the choir, of which I was a member. Now you talking about singing, child—we were *SANGING*. Ms. Miller could play the piano like nobody I had ever heard.

"My favorite songs are so numerous I couldn't pick just one," I told Thea-Thea enthusiastically.

"Sing 'Silent Night' for us, Baby Girl."

"Yes ma'am."

I began singing. By the time I got to "round yon virgin, mother and child," she had joined in with me. It was beautiful, two-part harmony.

I looked around at her, and she was crying. "Oh, Baby Girl, ya sang so beautifully. Ya gonna be something one of these days, I just know it."

Daddy said softly, "Ah boy, dat's mighty pretty, mighty pretty."

I had joined the choir after the cheerleading failure. So I had devoted my study hall period to music, which was my first love anyway.

The excitement in the school for the holiday was contagious. Preparing for the Christmas concert was simply enormous joy and celebration as we sang to the height of our abilities. It made the thought of the divine baby boy coming more exciting. It was as if He was going to be born and we were all going to be a part of His birth. We were going to sing for the KING! Even the boys in the choir were moist-eyed when we sang.

I wanted my friends to be a part of this beautiful singing, so I told my *posse* that they should all join the choir next year.

"Have you lost your ever loving mind?" squealed Carolyn. "I am not about to give up my study period to sing in no choir. That's about as boring as school itself. I'm sitting beside this cute guy every day, and he's giving me the eye. *Huh*, sing on, girl."

"I'll join, ClaraBy!" said Olive. "I love to sing, I just didn't think about it this year."

"Well, I said, I've got enough sense to know that I can study at home and sing in the choir too! That cute boy is probably dumb as a rock, but you go head on honey, do yo *thang*!"

The other girls just muttered something as I walked off thinking, *What a crock, I ain't following no losers.* This was much more beneficial to me than cutting off the legs of my pajamas.

So the day arrived for the concert. The boys in the choir had been busy making a shed for Mary, Joseph, and the baby Jesus. It was standing in the middle of the stage, which had been decorated to look like outdoors, with cardboard shepherds and sheep. It was creativity at its greatest.

There were three long steps for the choir to stand on behind the manger scene.

The girls were striking in our black skirts and white blouses, and the boys were really handsome in their black pants and white shirts.

Sacrifices had been made for some of us to have our uniforms. The home-economics class had been busy as bees making pants, shirts, and blouses. Even some of the women in the communities had made skirts and blouses and shirts.

The curtain opened. Oh my God! The gym was full of our parents, mostly mothers, and other people from school and its communities who were able to come. They were sitting in chairs on the floor, while the school kids were in the bleachers.

"Butterflies, butterflies!" Stephanie and I glanced at each other in awe. She was the girl next to me on my left. We were thrilled. We were getting ready to sing. And sing we did . . . .

After we got home from school that evening, sitting and talking, Junior said, "Baby Girl, I believe I could hear you over all of them."

"Really," I said.

"Yeah, I'm sure of it."

Ms. AnnaBelle, Ms. Maxwell, Ms. Ruth and Aunt Cellie were preparing a play for the church after Sunday school to be held on the Sunday before Christmas. We were beside ourselves with anticipation when we went to Sunday school that first Sunday in December, because they were choosing the main players and the extras. I was chosen to be one of the singing angels. I was sooooo excited.

Junior was chosen to play Joseph. He would be in his room rehearsing every night. He was really liking the acting thing.

Ms. Maxwell was making the baby out of brown cloth and dressed it in feed-sack cloth. She had even made the manger out of an old hog trough she had out back. By her habit of keeping everything she ever had, she made all of the costumes for the characters.

It was amazing when we went to church that Sunday, not really knowing what to expect except that she had told Ms. Ruth, Ms. AnnaBelle, and Aunt Cellie not to worry, just give her the number of costumes they would need.

Man, she was beaming with pride at her magnificent work, and so was everybody else. She took each character into the storage closet where all the wood, coal, and other stuff was kept and dressed us one by one. She had made the wings out of white feed-sack and sticks, and tied them around the ones playing the angels.

Magic, I tell you. I felt like an angel as I put on my costume. Oh, how I wished Ludie was able to come, she would have enjoyed it so much. I know, I thought brightly, I'll keep my angel costume on and go to see her after church and tell her all about it. Whatever was wrong with her was worsening. She could no longer get out of bed by herself.

The play was so beautiful. Candles were lit to give it a night appearance, and in came Joseph and Mary. Mary walked beside a cardboard donkey as Joseph led it. I was singing softly, "It Came Upon a Midnight Clear." Mrs. Francine was crying her eyes out.

"Oh, Ludie, I can't wait to tell you about it," I thought to myself. I so wished she could have been there to see how real it felt.

My brother Frank came to see the play, which was unusual to say the least, even though the older boys were raised up in the church, when they got grown, they stopped coming.

Thea-Thea had resigned to just praying "dat da Lawd would speak to their hearts, and I'm relying on da word dat says 'ya bring up a child in da way he should go, he knows da way and I know I's done my part. They'll come running back one of these days. I hope I be here to see it."

There is no place on earth that can compare to our community, and no other place I'd rather be during the Christmas holidays.

The Christmas play out of the way the Sunday before, left the week free to plan for the big day. The days leading up to Christmas Eve were so busy. I had long since found out that Santa Claus was not who I thought he was all those years. What a crock of . . . well . . . I was a little disappointed.

But I understood when my daddy told us boldly, "They ain't no such thang as Sandy Claus. I the only Sandy Claus ya ever had. Ain't no fat white man in no red suit worked not one day for ya."

He said he wanted to tell his "grandchilluns," but he would leave that up to their mom and dad. So I got to help hide their toys.

By now I don't know how many little gremlins my sis had; they were like popcorn it seemed. Year after year, after year . . . . They were all so cute, especially the big-eyed girls who looked up to me with such love that I returned gratefully, because they made me feel special. My brother took the boys as his *pets*, and they loved their uncle Junior with a passion. They would hardly let me even hold them if Junior was around. They adored him.

Now you talking 'bout some cooking going on in the camp during Christmas, yum, yum, yum. My Thea-Thea would turn the kitchen into a restaurant fit for a king, cooking everything that was imaginable.

Every house seemed to be busy. Ever so often, one of the women would come to the porch and holler up the hill for Thea-Thea.

Ms. Nellie hollered, "Hey, Thea-Thea, what ya doing now?"

Thea-Thea would holler back from the front porch, "Girl, I got my pies in da oven and beating my cake right now."

"Go'n girl, I'm doing my cakes too!"

Thea-Thea hollered down the hill at Ms. Francine, "Girl, what ya doing now?"

Ms. Francine hollered back, "Honey-child, them chittlins is talking, ya hear me, *talking*. Heee, heeee . . . I'll see ya later."

The men enjoyed this time of year to the max. They just lazed around coming in the kitchens, looking in the ovens and pots; the women would have to run them out. They were glad then, 'cause they'd make a big fire at the Crow Pole and drink and lie. They seemed to have so much fun. The children would be playing and praying that it would "snow real big, Lord!"

If a fresh snow had fallen, Thea-Thea would call all of us kids to come get some homemade snow ice cream. Oh, my goodness, you talking 'bout good. I tell you. Life is good . . . .

Ludie loved Christmas too, she was crocheting a shawl for me exactly like the one she wore. She was so proud. I was beaming at every stitch 'cause I knew she would finish it for Christmas, and I would be so tickled. Her hands were so frail and fragile and I know she was in pain, but she toiled on.

Thea-Thea let me get her a pretty gown from the company store. I was so excited wrapping it up. I wrapped it and unwrapped, and wrapped it again. Everything was going so beautifully. School was already out for the holidays.

The day before Christmas Eve, Thea-Thea and Junior were screaming: Russell had surprised us! He was on furlough for the holidays.

I ran down the stairs; my sister and the kids were running up the hill. Everybody was crying, I ran and jumped up in his arms.

"Oh God," I cried, "my Russell, my Russell!" It just so happened to be on a Friday and excitement was *already* in the air. The pots were *already* hopping. The cook stoves were red hot.

Thea-Thea had Russell's hand as if she would never let it go. It wasn't quite time for Daddy to come home, so he was going to be totally surprised to see Russell.

Junior was so overjoyed he was crying. He hugged Russell saying, "Man, I've missed you!"

Junior and I had long given up running to greet Daddy, as now we felt that we were past that stage. It was the grandchildren now, and Thea-Thea was doing the same thing for them, leaving some snacks in his lunch bucket for each one big enough to make the trip.

She actually had a second tin box that she loaded especially for Daddy to keep their snack. When Thea-Thea handed him his lunch bucket, the little tin box handle was strapped to the handle of his lunch bucket.

So when it was time for Daddy to come home, the big kids took off down the hill to greet him.

Russell hid upstairs, and when Daddy came in, we greeted him as usual, with hugs and kisses, and Junior's familiar pat on the head, and then a big-man handshake now that he was almost ready to graduate.

Big Sis had gone home with the little ones to get Mr. Man off to work.

Daddy did his usual thing—bathing and all!—and just as he emerged from behind the stove, Russell came down stairs, still in his uniform. Daddy almost fainted! He grabbed him up and actually cried with joy. It was a happy, happy, happy day for us.

That night, we stayed up almost all night talking and laughing. I took the little ones upstairs and played with them while the adults stayed downstairs. I had never seen my sister so happy. She seemed to be glowing with happiness. Well, she was glowing all right. Need I say more . . . ?

Daddy and my brothers had gone up in the woods and cut down the most beautiful tree. Thea-Thea and I decorated it while the men tried to put the toys that needed assembling together.

That Christmas Eve was the most wonderful time of my life. We wrapped the kids' presents, and Daddy, Mr. Man, Junior, and Russell had a ball trying to put the tricycle, bicycle, wagon, and other toys together.

Daddy stone sober couldn't read the instructions, but half-lit, he knew *everything* . . . if you know what I mean. He had wheels on backward and such. They would fall out laughing. He and Mr. Man were really having a drinking good time.

Finally, Russell and Junior ended up putting the toys together right.

Thea-Thea made me go to bed. The house would have somebody coming in and out all night. The men would come in and out to have a drink. The women would come to make a toast to the holiday, have a drink, and get right back to cooking. They really knew how to have a good time. Christmas was always happy, happy, *hap-py!*

It was almost midnight when we heard a car horn blowing. We all knew what that meant: someone was coming in from out of town. Thea-Thea said, "I wonder whose child dat is showing off in da middle of da night?"

I jumped out of bed and ran to the window to see what I could see.

We heard voices as Daddy opened the door to see if he could tell which house they was going to. Lo and behold, Ms. Nellie was hollering "THEA-THEA, THEA-THEA, CAL, CAL!"

It was Oscar!

"LAWD, LAWD, MY BABY, MY BABY!" Thea-Thea was screaming with house shoes on going down the steps. Big Sis came running out of the house. Oscar and Big Sis were hugging as they ran up the hill. Frank was so happy, he was crying. Oscar had written him and told him he would be in, but Frank had kept it to himself. Oscar pointed at him and said firmly, "I came to git you, bro." His car was loaded down with presents.

People started gathering at the house from the camp, especially the out-of-towners. They were all so glad to be together again. Now, our family was complete once more. Thank you dear, Lord. I went back to bed and never heard a thing that went on. I was *wore* completely out.

Christmas Day, I woke up to a quiet house, except for Thea-Thea making coffee. I flew down stairs to the Christmas tree to see what I had.

"Ooooooh!" I screamed as I opened present after present.

Russell had brought me the prettiest dress you have *everrrrrr* laid your eyes on. It was a deep dark red, with rows of black all around it. The skirt was full, and underneath was the most beautiful black can-can I have ever seen. He had brought black patent leather shoes and my very first pair of stockings.

Oscar had brought me this beautiful *leopard* coat with matching hat and hand muff! It was the most beautiful thing I had ever seen. I was speechless, and that's saying a lot. I was so excited I didn't know what to do. I screamed and screamed as I hugged them both. They really know how to treat a lady! I had so many presents. I was a happy child, you hear me.

Russell had brought presents for everybody; Thea-Thea had a brand new mixer. She was so excited, ready to make a cake. He bought Daddy new long johns and coveralls, Big Sis a pretty new coat, Junior new pants, shirts, and shoes. Everybody was happy. After all of my excitement, I asked to go to my Big Sis's to see the children and their gifts.

Oh my goodness, the joy in seeing them open their presents, fighting over the tricycle. Even the baby who could barely walk was trying to ride it. Paula stood back like a big girl and supervised, as the bike was hers. That was one thing about Mr. Man—he was just like my daddy when it came to his children.

My sis was cooking and singing along with somebody on the record player, "Bells will be ringing, please come home for Christmas, if not for Christmas, try New Year's night." She was so happy.

She grabbed me and started dancing with me around the kitchen. We giggled and giggled. The children were having a ball.

"Big Sis," I said, "I'm going to Ludie's to take her her gift."

"Okay, Baby Girl," she said.

I ran over to Ludie's, knocking on the door. Ms. Francine opens the door as I holler "Merry Christmas!" running past her to Ludie's room.

Ms. Francine had her looking so pretty sitting in the rocking chair by the Christmas tree, grinning from ear to ear. I ran to her with my gift. She was so excited, but very weak. She handed me my gift. Ms. Francine had wrapped it so beautifully, and even though I knew what it was, I was so excited, 'cause I knew that it was made with LOVE.

"Merry Christmas, Ludie!" I screeched.

"Open it for me ClaraBy," she said softly joyfully.

I took my time and opened the pretty wrapping with care. She was anxiously waiting.

She screeched as she pulled out the beautiful gown set that Thea-Thea had gotten for me to give her from the company store. They had special ordered it.

"Ooohhh, ClaraBy," she said, "it's so pretty, it's so dainty. Ooohhh," she kept saying, "Thank you . . . *God is so gooooood.*"

Mr. Cecil came in after about an hour and gently picked her up and placed her frail frame back in bed. Kissing her forehead he asked, "ain't ya ready to eat yet baby?" We got lots a goodies.

I stayed with her for hours, lying on the bed with my face in my hands, as she read me the story of Jesus' birth. She made it seem so real, as if this was the exact day.

* * *

The camp was full of people who had come home for Christmas. Children had come home from different places, and moms and dads were happy to see their babies—even though they were grown, they were still their babies.

Frank came down with presents, grinning from ear to ear, glad to be with his family. Margaret had left him a year and a half ago, and he was the most eligible bachelor in town, it seemed. He said he was never gonna live with "nary 'nother woman." He was one happy camper.

I thought as the day ended, *This has been a good day . . . . A GOOD DAY . . . . Thank you, LORD.*

Chapter Forty-Two

BACK TO THE NITTY GRITTY

Back in school after Christmas break, semester exams were near, and everyone was cramming—'cause these teachers didn't play, you hear me. You got it or else. Discipline was strict, and respect for teachers was high. They didn't take no junk, and God forbid if they had to call your parents or send a note home for anything that you had done wrong. You were doomed on both ends. Things had happened that as youngsters we seemed to not have paid much attention to, but it was exciting to know. One of the things was that a Negro woman had refused to give up her seat on the bus to a white man. Now that got my attention cause I suspect that if that had been me, I would have been that Negro woman, you see, I'm just that kinda gal with guts. I didn't remember what her name was at the time, just that she was one brave woman and all of the Negros were very proud of her.

Paddling was a weapon of *ass-destruction*, and they were not afraid to use it, with the blessings of every parent, and if you were unfortunate to receive a paddling, you got another one when you got home. Thank God, I never received one, 'cause Thea-Thea would have surely killed me when I got home. Junior was a good boy too, as he knew she didn't play, and God forbid if Daddy was the one to do the whooping.

My two oldest brothers had told of the time when they were grown but still living at home, working in the coal mines. They shared the same bed, and one night they were tussling over the cover, one saying the other had it all on their side, and then the other, the argument ensued, the tussling continued.

"Well," Oscar said, "Daddy solved the problem real quick with his mining belt, saying, "When ya live under my roof, ya go by my rules; if ya don't like it, ya know what ya can do." The next week, they both moved out.

That was just the way it was in the black-coal fields. You respected your parents and your elders—I don't care if it was the camp drunk.

* * *

The school year was nearing an end. Junior and I both making the honor roll twice. He was so proud of himself—as we all were—as it was his first time ever making the honor roll.

He said, "Baby Girl, I think I'll join the army too after I graduate. Russell says that I can further my education in the armed services, and I'm thinking about being a doctor or something like that . . . . What you think of that?"

I said, "I think you got your ducks in a row, big brother—go for it."

"What you want to be when you grow up, Baby Girl?"

I said, "Oh, I don't know; sometimes I think I want to be a nurse, and then I think I want to sing, and then I think, well, I . . . I just haven't made up my mind yet."

"Well," he said, "it's time you started thinking ahead, 'cause next year, you'll be a sophomore."

We walked up the road behind the other kids just talking in general. It was really good. We were really close.

Chapter Forty-Three

NOT MY LUDIE, LORD!

Thea-Thea was standing on the porch, as were the other mothers, which was not unusual, but this day, it seemed a little strange. No one was laughing and talking. We spoke to everyone as we passed.

I glanced at Ludie's house saddened by the fact that she would never be able to sit on the porch it seemed ever again. Daddy hadn't gone to work that day, as he wasn't feeling well. We were coming up the steps, when Daddy said, "Come here, Baby Girl."

"Yes sir?" I said. "What's wrong, Daddy?"

He said, "Baby Girl, I got some bad news."

"What Daddy? I asked, my heart racing 'cause I didn't know what was wrong! I saw the kids and my Big Sis on the porch, everybody seemed all right. So what was wrong?

He said, "Baby Girl, you know Ludie has been very sick, and . . ."

"Ooooooh Nooooooooo!" I screamed. "Noooooo, Nooooooooo. Not my Ludie, Daddy, Not my Ludie!"

He wrapped his arms around me. He didn't have to tell me anymore, I just knew she was gone. I cried and cried and cried. Thea-Thea fixed me some hot tea and told me to drink it. My head was hurting so bad.

"Ooooh, Thea-Thea," I cried.

"I know, my child, I know," she said, "but she was soooo sick. Da Lawd just said 'enough suffering, my child, come on home and rest.' She went peacefully in her sleep. Francine said she went into her room this mo'ning to check on her bout 9 o'clock and she was gone. She said she had checked on her bout 2 o'clock an she was sleeping peacefully, so she went back to bed.

I cried and cried. I couldn't forget Ludie telling me, just the day before, that she would always be with me no matter what. Her little voice was so soft, I had to hold my head down close to her to hear her talk. Lying in that big bed, looking so pretty.

Oh God, what am I going to do without my Ludie? She had whispered to me just yesterday, "Whenever you have a problem, just remember to take it to God, and I'll be there smiling."

"Oooh Ludie," I cried as I finally fell asleep.

The next morning, Thea-Thea gave me a choice to go to school or not. I chose to go, because I knew Ludie would have wanted me to. She had always told me to be brave and hold my head high. She would say, "ClaraBy, someday you're gonna shake up the world!"

I'd say, "Yeah, right!"

"No," she said, "I mean it! You can do anything you set your mind to. You just have to set your mind to it . . . . Don't forget to read the scriptures . . . and stay in church . . . keep on singing; even when you feel like crying, sing yourself out of fear," she said, "I do." I blew a kiss at her window as I passed by that morning. My heart was heavy, but my determination was strong.

I went to see Ms. Francine after school. She was so hurt. It was hard to see her mourning. She and Mr. Cecil were devastated.

"Ooooh, ClaraBy, she loved ya so much," she said.

I didn't know what to say, so I just sat with them in the kitchen and talked. Later on, Ms. Francine and I went into Ludie's room. I had a big lump in my throat; I just didn't know what to do. Ludie was gone. Ludie was gone forever. I couldn't believe it. I kept looking at the bed, which was made up so beautifully. Everything was so pretty in her room. It *was* her.

Ms. Francine went to the dresser and opened the top drawer saying, "ClaraBy, Ludie wanted me to give this to ya at this time, and she wanted ya to open it right away.

She handed me an envelope with my name on it, in Ludie's handwriting. I remembered the poem she had written me. I had it in my dresser drawer, in a safe place.

Cora L. Hairston

I opened the envelope and read:
ClaraBy, be strong. Remember everything I've told you. You are a big girl now, so live. Live!"
This is a song I wrote. You sing it like you want to.

"I BELIEVE IN THE TOWN OF BETHLEHEM . . .
TO MARY AND JOSEPH, A MALE CHILD WAS BORN . . .
HE WAS BORN TO TAKE AWAY THE SINS OF THE WORLD . . .
BORN TO SAVE EVERY MAN, WOMAN, BOY AND GIRL . . .
LYING IN A MANGER, WRAPPED IN SWADDLING CLOTHES . . .
I BELIEVE . . . I BELIEVE . . .

I BELIEVE HE SAID, "LAZARUS, COME FORTH" . . .
AND HE RAISED LAZARUS FROM THE DEAD . . .
I BELIEVE 5000 HUNGRY SOULS HE FED . . .
WITH 2 FISHES, AND 5 LOAVES OF BREAD . . .
AND THE WOMAN WITH THE ISSUE OF BLOOD,
I BELIEVE HE HEALED HER . . .
I BELIEVE . . . I BELIEVE . . .

I BELIEVE . . . I BELIEVE . . . I BELIEVE . . . I BELIEVE . . .
I BELIEVE . . . I BELIEVE EVERY WORD . . . I BELIEVE . . .

I BELIEVE HE SUFFERED, BLED AND DIED . . .
AND IN THE GARDEN OF GETHSEMANE I BELIEVE HE CRIED . . . OUT
"NOT MY WILL, BUT THINE BE DONE" . . .
TO HIS FATHER FROM HIS ONLY BEGOTTEN SON . . .
AND OUT THERE ON THE CROSS OF CALVARY
I BELIEVE HE HUNG OUT THERE FOR ME . . .
I BELIEVE . . . I BELIEVE . . .

HERE'S ANOTHER THING . . .
I BELIEVE HE ROSE, AND HE'S COMING BACK AGAIN . . .
HE ROSE WITH ALL POWER IN HIS HANDS . . .
THE ANGEL WILL PLACE ONE FOOT UPON THE LAND AND
    ONE UPON THE SEA . . .

FROM THE CLOUD JESUS WILL CALL UP YOU AND ME
AND FOREVER, AND EVER, AND EVER,
WITH HIM WE WILL BE . . . OOOHHH, I BELIEVE, I BELIEVE . . .

Sing it like you mean it! Until then—remember, I love you—
TUDDIE LUDIE"

"Ooooh, Ms. Francine," I cried. She wrapped me in her arms, and we cried together.

Ms. Francine flopped down in Ludie's rocking chair and moaned. She was heartbroken. I sat on the bed and let her get herself together. Finally she said with a smile, "Ya gotta git home for school tomorrow, so off ya go little girl!"

"Yes ma'am," I said.

"We'll see ya tomorrow right?"

"Yes ma'am." I thought she felt that she was losing me too. I reassured her with a big hug and said, "I'll see you tomorrow. Good night Mr. Cecil."

"Good night child, be careful." He looked so thin and withered, as if the life had been sucked out of him. Ludie was his heart.

So off I went, walking very slow, crying every step of the way.

Thea-Thea, Daddy and Junior were standing on the porch watching me come up the road. Sorrow written all over their face, and concern for me.

"Come on in Baby Girl, let me fix ya a good hot cup a tea so ya can rest."

"Yes ma'am.

It was so hard attending her funeral. I was almost fifteen years old, and death was somewhat new to me, even though I had attended funerals before, but not my Ludie's. It just didn't seem fair. She never had a chance. I began to ask God, "Why? What am I to do without my Ludie?"

But then I remembered that she had read to me in the Bible that He would never leave me nor forsake me. I began to pray, "Lord, help me through this; it's so hard!" My body was weak with sorrow. I felt so limp. I felt so lonely.

And it seemed as if He whispered, "I know, my child . . . I'm with you, and I'll never leave you."

I sat with the family during the funeral. Ms. AnnaBelle sang,

No more trouble and sadness, no more trouble and sadness, I'm going home to live with my King . . . .

She sang that song with her head thrown back, looking up in the rafters as if she could see heaven.

The whole church was in mourning. Even though it had been expected, it just seemed so unreal. I was beside myself with grief. My Ludie, my Ludie. I just didn't want to think that I would not see her sitting on the porch again, nor would she ever say, "Where have you been all of my life?" *Oh Lord, I know You know how I feel. Please help me?*

Sitting there somewhat in shock, I got up out of my seat and went and stood in front of Ludie's coffin. I hadn't planned on singing the song she had written, but I had gone over it, over and over and over. The tune of the song just seemed to come to me. It was as if I *had* to sing it.

So I did.

I was so hurt, I didn't think anything else could be worse. Boy, was I wrong. Little did I know that in my young life, heartaches and heartbreaks were just beginning.

We left the church singing, "Some glad morning when this life is over, I'll Fly Away." . . . It was such a melodious sound that it seemed as though Ludie herself was flying above us. I sang as loud as I could as we went over the hill from the church to the little cemetery. It was just like Ludie to have a beautiful spring day for her funeral. So what else is new.

* * *

Well, I made it through the rest of the school year. School helped a lot to ease the pain of losing my very best friend. Ludie had lived to see a brand new year come and although March had come in like a lion, spring had sprung and it was showing signs of warmth and beauty. But my heart ached that she would not be here to see another anything.

I was beginning to be interested in boys, and one boy in particular I had my eyes on. and, quite a few boys had their eyes on me.

Losing Ludie seemed to open my eyes to real life. I had not experienced a death so close to my heart. I grew up during that time it seemed. I felt that Ludie had been here for a purpose, for a short time, and she had fulfilled that purpose. I felt that she was sent here as my guardian angel. It made me feel good to think that she was watching my every move from heaven. I had better be good as I felt her saying, "Now, little girl, what is your mission? Are you going to waste it, or are you going to make it happen?"

Yes, Ludie, I'm going to make it happen!

Chapter Forty-Four

GROWING UP, *UH-OH*

The summer was quite an interesting summer. I spent part of it in Virginia, where I met this gorgeous black—and I do mean gorgeous—*black* boy. It was not as if it was for the first time, it was just that it was the first time we really, really noticed each other. *Theodore* was the sixth or seventh child of the brood of fourteen children of the Spencer family. *Yes,* I thought, *this is going to be an interesting year that will change my life forever.*

The adult church group held sock hops on Saturday nights up on High Street in a little place for the younger kids. Theodore and I danced side by side to the Stroll, the Madison, the Cha-Cha, and other dances. No slow love songs were played, as boys and girls were not allowed to be in close contact. I mean, those old ladies watched us teenagers like hawks! They did not play when it came to you being respectful.

We always had fun walking home afterward. Theodore would hold my hand as we walked. Sometimes we would run, and he would grab me and swing me around. *Oh,* he was sooo handsome.

Promptly at nine o'clock p.m., it was all over, and you had better be home by 9:15 . . . unless you had a broken leg and on crutches . . . or else you might end up with a *broke* neck.

My aunt Idella didn't play. But my cousin Katherine was a little on the . . . uh . . . uh . . . *fast* side . . . . She always managed to get home on time, but not without doing a little hanky-panky along the way.

One Saturday night after one of our social events, we were in the bedroom talking soft and low, and she told me *all about it*, saying, "Girl, you don't know what you missing. Do you think Theo's gonna stick around with you just giving up a kiss? Heck no," she said.

"Well," I said, "he had better kiss where the sun don't shine, 'cause that's all he's gonna get from me, and if you don't stop, you're gonna end up being visited by the 'Big Bird.' Heee, heeeee, and then, you are on your own, Honey Child, 'cause Joe? Huh, he's gonna drop you like a hot poe-tay-*toe*! Mark my word."

"Uh, uhmm," she said, "me and Joe know what we doing."

Well, she told me all about *everything*. I was like "Wow, it does sound verrrry interesting, but my Thea-Thea says if you let a boy get on top of you, you'll get visited by the 'Big Bird,' and your life is ruined forever, and the boy is gone on about his business she says, and I don't intend to let no boy ruin my changes in the big time, no sirree!" I said.

"Oh, for God's sake, stop it!" she screeched softly. "You know they don't know how to control themselves—look at 'em—all they do is *just do it;* they don't know nothing else. Now, me and Joe, we know what we doing . . . . You curious, and done felt like it . . . you just chicken," she said, falling back on the bed.

"Chicken, smicken, I ain't gonna try it till I'm good and ready, and I sho' ain't ready now. I'm gonna stay pure as the driven snow until I am Mrs. Theodore Spencer."

Well, that settles that, I thought, *I'm outa here!* It was getting a little bit too hot in Virginia.

"You're not going to stay for your birthday? Girl, we was gonna throw you a party. What's wrong with you?"

"No. I would, but I told Aunt Cellie I would help her do her windows. So I had better get back home before I spend all my summer doing nothing and then have to do it when school starts back up." I was trying to make any excuse I could to get the hell outa Dodge before things got even hotter. And after a month, I left to go back home, because Aunt Idella was acting a little suspicious, and I didn't want my Thea-Thea to get suspicious of me. So home I went on the big bus.

I was well informed about the facts of life through my cousin's informative lips, and I wasn't about to let my hormones get in my way, because Theodore was so fine and it was so haaaarrdd to resist. I had to get out of there quick, and I do mean *quick*.

Big Mama was watching us like a hawk. Theodore could only come to the house for an hour in the evening after we had finished our chores. We had to sit in the living room on the couch—with Big Mama sitting in the big chair across from us crocheting and whistling softly, "Yield Not to Temptation." When the hour was up, I would walk him to the door, and that was when we would get our kiss on.

"Ooooooooh my God, it was so sweet . . . his lips were so soft . . . and his, his, well, his, well . . . . Oh my GOD! I've GOT to go home!

Chapter Forty-Five

CHANGE IS COMING

Things seemed to be changing in the hollow. The coal mine where Daddy worked was doing poorly. Men were being laid off left and right. People were moving to different parts of the state looking for work. The water supply had gotten very low.

Aunt Cellie had moved out of the hollow down the road about five miles, just above the middle school.

She was so tickled. "I done found me a good man, she told Thea-Thea. He works in the mines, and his ole lady done left him for another man and took his two kids wit her. Well, if it's one thang I know, it's how to treat a man, 'specially one dat's working and bringing da check home and giving it to me. Haaaa, I gonna hold on. Long as he knows I ain't one to be beat on and not one to be cheated on. Treat me right, ya got a friend. Yes indeed-eeeee!!" Another thang, I done already tol him, I don't live wit no man unless he all mine, so git them papers, git divorced an git da preacher ready. Hee, heeee."

She now lived in a busy community that had more houses all around, stores and juke joints. There was a lot of action going on, and that was right up her alley. She said she had never been so happy. She lived out back in the house that Mr. Moore had built with his own hands. The summer was passing slowly it seemed. I had to go down to Aunt Cellie's one Saturday to help her clean windows.

I must say, as a young lady, I had blossomed quite nicely. It was a very hot early August summer day, so I had worn my short-shorts to work in. I was very particular about the way I looked, so I had taken much pain in getting dressed that day. Thea-Thea had Mr. Judd drop me off at the car bridge to walk down the camp to Aunt Cellie's house. He would come back and pick me up when he came back from downtown, which he said would be around seven o'clock.

"Yes, sir," I said as I thanked him, getting out of the car.

Going across the bridge, walking down the first half of the community, it seemed so busy. Everyone was on their porch sweeping, or just sitting. I was politely speaking to everyone.

Just as I began my turn to go down the back alley to Aunt Cellie's, I heard some whistles and wolf calls coming from down the camp. I looked down the road, and on one of the porches I saw four or five men—or boys, I couldn't tell which as I was not trying to oblige them with noticing them—so I kept walking. I continued down the alley to Aunt Cellie's house, which sat off to itself behind a row of houses.

Aunt Cellie had decorated the house so cute, and it was spotless. She gave me a bucket of vinegar water and some rags to wash the outside windows.

I began to wash the windows on the front of the house outside, singing to myself, when someone came up behind me and said, "Hey, what's yo name?"

I thought, *I swanny* . . . as I replied, "Puddin' Tang, ask me again and I'll tell you the same."

"You sure do fill those shorts out nicely," he said.

I turned slowly and said, "You low down blankety-blank-blank..." I continued to tell him off without any thought of slowing down. He looked like that little dog that walks the camp that everybody feeds, but I didn't stop.

He finally said, "I . . . I . . . I'm sorry, I didn't mean to upset you. I just didn't' know what to say . . . I saw you and I thought—"

"Well," I said, "who gave you any reason to think that you could bring your sorry ass over here and say such a thing to me? You don't know me, and I don't know you, and further more, I *don't want* to know you—so go further and smell better, and take your thoughts with you and get the—"

"Well!" said Aunt Cellie, coming out of the house. "Hi, Mark, how are you?"

"I'm fine, Ms. Cellie," the dummy replied.

I was still seething, washing windows like mad ignoring him as she talked.

"I see ya met my niece," she said.

"Well, not exactly," he said.

Aunt Cellie said, "Mark, this is my niece, ClaraBy; ClaraBy, this is Mark Powell; he lives up da street a piece."

He replied by saying, "I thought she said her name was Puddin' Tang," trying to be smart.

I rolled my eyes at him in disgust.

Aunt Cellie, not knowing what had just taken place, laughed and said, "Mark, she not one to play wit, so ya had better 'proach softly. She can—"

"Aunt Cellie, please," I said, "I can handle this, if you don't mind?"

I turned to him and handed him the rag and bucket of vinegar water I was washing windows with and said, "Make yourself useful."

He ended up cleaning all of the windows inside and out—and there were a lot of windows. I drank lemonade and did not offer him any. I just let him work his butt off, dying laughing inside.

Chapter Forty-Six

THE BIG MOVE

School started, and it was so chaotic. It was buzzing everywhere about *integration!* We were given the option to attend the white high school or to stay at Bulldog High. Well, some of us who had been in school together all through the nine years were undecided. We all wanted to stay together and graduate together, but curiosity was getting to some of us. Some of us were deciding to go, and then would suddenly change our minds. It went back and forth. Some of the black teachers had already been placed in some of the white schools, like it or not.

The school system seemed to think it was a step up, as we would have access to new books instead of the hand-me-downs we got now, but it seemed a big price to pay leaving Bulldog High. So, after careful thought, some of us decided to go to the big school that sat all alone past the football field. We would always see the school when we played football, but were never allowed to even dream about attending. But here it was, the "Big Moment," the "Big Move." Some of us went with enthusiasm, and some of us went with a heavy heart. It wasn't a matter of *if* you wanted to, as we were told Bulldog High was going to be integrated too. So, "What the heck," we said. Off we went.

It was terrifying that first day. The school was huge by Bulldog High standards. We stayed to ourselves, but as it ended up, only a couple of my friends from Bulldog High were in the same homerooms or classes anyway.

We were looked at as if we had leprosy or something. Nobody, and I do mean *nobody* was friendly. Not even the teachers.

Luckily, I got in the homeroom of one of the black teachers from Bulldog High. He was a handsome man who walked tall and took no junk from nobody. I felt so much better when I walked into the classroom and saw it was Mr. Rolllins. I took my seat feeling much better. We were assigned classes, and the chaos began.

It was a hard transition, as racism was something that we were not used to. Every race always seemed to keep to themselves, but now, we were together, and it wasn't going smoothly.

Some of the black boys seemed to do okay though, Junior included. As it turned out, that was because they were the football stars from Bulldog High.

The days and weeks passed so slowly, and little by little, some of the white kids kind of warmed up, but not much. One morning in particular, our bus arrived on campus, and there was a dummy that had been tarred, feathered, and hung on the lower part of the flag pole and then set on fire. Some white kids were doing an "Indian" dance around it in a circle, as other white kids looked on laughing and enjoying the stunt. The black kids were just standing around looking, not doing anything.

I couldn't stand it any longer. Junior grabbed my arm, but I jerked away and joined in with them—I started to do the same as they were doing. When they realized that I was in the circle, they stopped and looked at me as if I were crazy.

I looked at them as if to say, "WHAT? WHAT!" My right eyebrow was raised, and they knew from the look on my face that I wasn't there to take no shh . . . stuff. The bell rang, and they drifted off.

We went to class without any incident, and nothing was ever said about it anymore. The teachers all knew what had happened, but they pretended that it hadn't. The next morning when our bus arrived, everyone was hurrying inside, no one was lingering. Junior said, "Baby Girl, please make sure you don't cause no trouble, 'cause they'll be watching you."

"I won't, Junior. If they don't start none, there won't be none."

"I'm just down the hall if you need me, okay?"

"Okay," I replied as I hurried to my homeroom.

One of the popular white girls in my homeroom, a petite thing that dripped with the look of money, passed my desk and leaned down and said, "That was a very brave thing you did yesterday."

"Yeah, well," I said, "I just don't like nobody making fun of anybody, especially me." She was one of the nice ones and a cheerleader too. The other white kids had kept their heads down when I came into the room.

Mr. Rollins called the roll. When the bell rang for the first period, I was gathering my books and things, and he called me up to his desk, "Listen, little girl, I don't want no mess out of you. You mind your Ps and Qs," he said.

"Yes sir," I said as I hurried out.

The black boys were kind of laid back, they didn't make no waves at all. Some of the black girls though, were a different story, especially me and Olive.

There was a snack bar off-campus, and a bus terminal. Some of the white kids would go to the snack bar on their lunch break and dance. So Olive and I decided that we wanted to go. The other black boys and girls went to the little snack bar owned by Mr. Gardner (a black man), which was much farther away from campus There was a juke box there, but no dancing space.

So off we went giggling and running. We had never been there, as most of our posse from Bulldog High would go to the bus terminal. We were in awe looking around not knowing what to expect or what to do. It was huge! Much, much nicer than Mr. Gardner's.

Everyone turned and looked at us as we entered. We felt a little uncomfortable, as it was a very akward moment. We spoke softly to one of the girls that we recognized. She looked shocked, never replying. It was like we were aliens or something. They were looking at us as if we had just landed. *Duh.*

The ones on the dance floor were just standing there when another record dropped. Olive and I knew all of the latest dances, so we started dancing with each other. We did the Stroll, the Twist, the Madison, and the Cha-Cha. The white kids didn't know any of the dances, so they were doing what they do, looking at us, and whispering to each other. We didn't pay them any mind; we just kept on dancing when the songs would change. The person spinning the records played all of the latest hits, so it was fun. Nobody bothered us; they just didn't know what to do, I guess.

Finally, one of the girls came over between dances and asked if we would teach her the dance. "Sure thing," we replied gladly. The ice was broken. They wanted to learn, and we were happy to teach them.

Well, after a few days of fun and dance, me and Olive went running to the snack bar to get our dance on. But this day, some man was standing in the doorway and wouldn't let us in. He let the white kids pass, but when we attempted to pass, he stepped in front of us, spread his legs, and told us we couldn't come in.

"Why not," I asked?

"Because I said so," he replied.

Well, I just followed the next bunch of white kids, and called for Olive. He moved aside, as red as a beet, and let her pass.

As soon as we got back to school and were in class, the PA system came on and someone clearing their throat said, "ClaraBy Mickens, Olive Leonard: REPORT TO THE PRINCIPAL'S OFFICE."

Everyone in the room turned and looked at me. The teacher buried her head in something she was pretending to look at on her desk. The rumor had preceded us before lunch was over, so they knew what was coming.

I met up with Olive as she came out of her room. We didn't know what was wrong, but we had a pretty good idea.

"Oh my goodness, ClaraBy, we're in trouble."

"For what, I wonder?"

We got to the principal's office, and Mr. Rushden raked us over the coals. He expelled us! We had to call our parents to come get us. We couldn't even ride the bus home, so we had to find a way as best we could. But old, faithful Mr. Judd had been contacted and came and picked us up and took us home. He had long since gotten rid of his truck as he's retired now, and had a nice car.

The camp was all abuzz about the issue. Everybody was on the telephone, which was a party line, so you just picked up the phone if you were fortunate enough to have one, and joined in the conversation.

Integration was already a tough row to hoe for Southern black parents who were used to working with or for whites for a number of hours and then going home, but not so for their children, whom they had to send off alone thinking *God only knows what they're facing.* So nerves were really frayed now with the thought of two of their girls having been traumatized for trying to fit in. Also, now me and Olive had gone and rocked the boat and feeling very guilty like we had committed the unforgiveable sin and messed up everything for all of the black kids.

I was really worried about Olive. Here again, I had led her astray! I knew she was going to be in for it. And I was scared to death for myself, not knowing what Daddy and Thea-Thea would do to me. So I had to get my story straight. As the car entered the hollow, I swallowed hard and looked at Olive.

"Well, here goes," she said.

Big Sis came out on the porch and asked if I was all right.

"Yes, I'm all right," I said sadly.

"I'll be up there in a minute," she said.

"Okay."

Thea-Thea was fit to be tied when I told her the whole story from start to finish. "A prejudiced bastard! The chilluns got mo' guts than any of 'em," she said, totally on my side. Whee, thank You Jesus!"

I had been so scared that I was going to be in trouble, but Daddy said, "I's proud of ya, Baby Girl. He shoulda been up front an honest wit ya from da start, 'stead he let ya teach dem kids how to do da dances, den ban ya. I's rather know what kinda man I's dealing wit up front; den I know how to handle him, 'cause he puts his pants on just like me, and I'll let him know it . . . . Ya just gitting a taste of what's to come in da world ya live in," Daddy said. "Stand yo grounds when ya right, and don't back down." Daddy went on to say, "It's tough enough for ya kids being snatched out of yo school an now being made fun of and picked on. *Don't take it*. I gota good mind to go down thar' myself."

"No! No! Cal! Thea-Thea said forcefully. We'll handle it. Go on to work."

Junior said, "I'm sorry I wasn't there for you, Baby Girl. But if this don't turn out right, I'll tell the rest of the boys, and we'll walk off the football team—and see how they like that. They ain't won a game in umpteen years, and if they think they're gonna use us to get them a championship, and then treat us like slaves, they got another think coming. I love football, but I ain't planning on making no living on it, so what the *hay?"* He was livid.

"RIGHT ON, BROTHER!" I said.

"I hate I'm graduating this year," he said, cause you've got two more years of this. But I'll see that you don't get picked on. We've got to stick together. I'll talk to the other guys tomorrow."

"Junior, be careful," Thea-Thea said, cause they particularly hard on young black boys—just look at what they did to dat poor fo'teen year old black boy down south. Lord, I tell ya, I don't know what this world is coming to. But I know one thang, Thea-Thea said, putting her hands on her hips, they ain't gonna use my child for no scapegoat. I'll be there in da morning wit bells on, and he had better know how to treat us mothers like ladies—don't he ain't seen nothing. I's hot as a stove right now, he don't know who he fooling wit, well, he gitting ready to find out."

Thea-Thea went on, "I'm gonna go down da hill and talk to Mable to see if she's gonna go on behalf of Olive. I believe she gon' be just as ready as I am. Y'all know dat meeting dat was held at church wit da chilluns and they parents. Well, weren't nobody happy wit this integration thang, 'cause we know from experience how snakes crawl." Pulling her apron off and laying it on the back of the chair, she marched out the door.

"Oh Lord," Junior said, laughing, I wish I could be a fly on the wall for this conversation. Mr. Rushden is in for a rude awakening."

Well, needless to say, Mr. Rushden (the principal), was gonna get a taste of the "YOU DON'T KNOW WHO YOU MESSING WITH WHEN

YOU MESS WITH A BLACK WOMAN'S CHILD," in living color. Heeeeeee, Heeeeeeeeee.

Mr. Judd drove Thea-Thea, Ms. Mable, Olive and me to school the next day. We weren't allowed in the office where the meeting was taking place, but we were in the outer office area and had good eye and earshot of what was going on.

Mr. Rushden, the assistant principal, and the owner of the snack bar were with our two, very mad, black mothers, who had strutted into that office that morning. Ms. Mable was leading the way—hat, gloves, and all.

Mr. Rushden was sitting behind the desk and the other men were sitting on his left with their legs crossed. He had some more chairs brought into the office so everyone was sitting as he cleared his throat and said in a very husky voice, "Everybody knows why we're here. We've got a problem with these girls bulldozing their way into the snack bar yesterday and I—"

"Just a minute 'fore ya go any further.'" He turned red as a beet when Ms. Mable interrupted him. "Now I's not one to talk much, but my granddaughter tol' me ya was not too nice yes'aday." Now I don't take kindly to dat . . . Ya see, my child 'splained to me what happened, and I believe her. She said ya took da side of him," and she pointed to the man who owned the place, "and didn't give dem a chance to 'splain.

His head snapped up as he was looking down at some paper he had before him. He wasn't expecting these bold black women.

She kept right on talking, saying, "It seems to me dat there was one of dem *secret meetings*, and it was decided dat they won't welcome no mo'. Well, ya shoulda told 'em when they first come dat they won't welcome. I sho' believe they wouldna come back. But no, ya did it underhanded, and I don't 'preciate it, not nary bit."

Ms. Mable went on to say, "Now I speck ya owe 'em an apology, but ya know what I expect is dat ya thank ya too good to apologize to a *Negro*. So don't bother. It ain't accepted no ways."

Then my Thea-Thea spoke up and said, very properly, "Rush." (shortening Mr. Rushden's name.) Now that really got his attention. He cleared his throat loudly as if that meant something.

But she continued by saying, "There ain't nothing no lower than three white men who thank dat, 'cause ya run thangs, ya gonna treat my child like she's a piece of *dung*. I know y'all run in packs like wolves, 'cause ya ain't man enough to stand by yo'self, but I tell ya true: don't mess wit my baby . . . . There ain't nothing in this world dat I would die for other than my chilluns. So I'm here to let ya know dat. If y'all doing yo job right, we wouldn't be here, 'cause my child said dat they had been going up to dat place for a while, and then all of a sudden, *You*," she said, pointing to the man that owned the little snack bar, "decide they can't come no mo'.

"Now," she continued. "I don't thank of ya as no man; I thank of ya as a prejudiced *racehorse* who thanks he too good to ride ever'body, so he throws who he wants off. Well, ya had better know I ain't sending my child here to be mistreated. Da thang for ya to do is apologize too.

But, she went on to say, "I don't expect it from ya, 'cause you thank you better than us . . . . Well, I got *news* for ya: ya ain't. We didn't ask for this *integration* thang, ya did, now live wit it, they here, and they gonna stay."

She turned and looked at Mr. Rushden and said, "Now dat's my boy you using on da football field to make a name for yo'self, 'cause ya couldn't do it yo'selves. Well, da girls just as important, if not mo' than da boys . . . . Now, if I have to come back down here for anythang concerning my chilluns, it had better be a darn good *ligit* reason. So let it be written, so let it be done.

"And as for you," she said, turning in her chair to look the owner straight in the face, "don't ya ever say a word to my child again in this life and beyond. As I said befo', (speaking real soft), there ain't nothing to me mo' worth dying for, so I know ya git da message of how dat goes—if I go, I ain't gonna go easy—somebody gonna go wit me, and dat ain't no threat, dat's a promise . . . . I know you wouldn't want the nation to hear about dis would ya? I'll call in da NAACP so fast, it'll make yo head swim. We'll pull a march ya ain't never seen befo', right here."

Ms. Mable was looking at her hands as she rubbed her fingers together, sucking her teeth. "Ya know," she said, "I's fought off men like ya all my life—ya want what ya want, when ya want it, how ya want it. I worked for one of ya rotten a-holes, always dodging his hand when his wife weren't looking, fighting ya off sometimes, allowing it sometimes to keep my job. But when da missus was around, ya turned; ya try to boss me round.

"I still see da sorry dog right today: he hangs his head when he sees me. Ya know why? Da day dat I quit, I had refused to allow him to touch me any-mo', and he accused me of stealing five dollars. Well, I went off on his sorry butt and told his wife everthang. I even told her of a birthmark dat only she knowed he had. Heeee, heeee, she left his sorry behind. I'll be damn if ya will do my child any harm, in or out of school. As a matter of fact, who works for ya as yo maid? I bet if I ask her, she got da same story to tell about you, yeah, I know yo type . . . . Now, my child is sitting out there, da skinny light-skinned one wit da red hair. Her name be Olive Spencer—remember it, and ever time ya hear it, know I's behind it. They gonna go to class now, and I want a copy of any and everthang dat ya done placed on da records, and I want it *now!*" And she stood and pounded on the desk.

Mr. Rushden stammered around and said that they only wanted to discuss the fact that we had forced our way into the snack bar, but that "it wasn't that big of a deal, is it Mr. Vance?"

"No, no, Mr. Rushden, it was simply a misunderstanding. We don't want no trouble out of you people," he said.

"'Misunderstanding!' repeated Thea-Thea. "*You people,*" she said softly, "now ya showing yo true self. "*You people* . . ." she said again, "This is da product of *yo* doing. We was doing just fine, but noooo, ya wanted to *intergrate*, give us da same education. Well, do yo job! They here now and they ain't going nowhere! So git over it! And as for them forcing their way in, they tell me dat you stood in da way, letting da white kids by and blocking them from going in. Now to me, dat is what ya call, uh—what's dat big word they using now days?—dis . . . dis . . . oh yeah, *discrimination*. Maybe we ought to call in the feds and see how they feel about ya letting them in to teach, but then not 'llowing them to enjoy da benefits of their labor . . . . Let's put this county on da prejudice map it 'spose be on! We don't teach our chilluns to be disrespectful to nobody, but we do teach them how *not* to be disrespected by *NOBODY*.

"It seems to me dat da girls da ones wit da *balls* in this room. Real men who ain't blinded by fear could see dat these girls was just trying to fit into a system dat y'all designed."

Ms. Mable spoke up and said, "My husband is gone be a minister. Fact is, he just preached his first sermon last Sunday. He preached 'bout a man who died for us all. Thank God *he* color blind, 'cause yo asses would be in trouble. Remember this, he da preacher, I ain't.

"Good day, gentlemen, and may God give ya wisdom and strength for da days and years ahead, 'cause, ya got a rough row to hoe. We will see ya again, 'cause anythang going on down here, we wanna know—meetings and such. Ya know what I mean, them meetings when ya meet wit they teachers."

Mr. Rushden tried to get a word in by saying, "Now listen here, ma'am, we . . . uh, uh, uh . . ."

"Watch what ya gonna say," Ms. Mable said with two fingers pointing toward him. "Ya ain't no young man, and you's got to face yo maker one of these days, and I'm sho' ya don't want to stand 'fore Him wit somethang like this to give in account for, cause I knows y'all fine *Christian*, Bible-toting men, ain't ya; go to church ever time da door open. So let's just chalk it up to ignorance. We understand."

Our mothers stood up at the same time and walked proudly out of the office and went to the window and asked the secretary for our papers.

Mr. Rushden was totally upset at the way the women had presented themselves, but he didn't say anything else. He pushed his chair back rather abruptly, and he and the other men came in behind the window from the other side mumbling something, their faces as red as beets.

The assistant principle gave the secretary instructions. We were told to go back to class. Our mothers instructed us, individually and together, that we had better not cross any lines.

Thea-Thea told us in no uncertain terms that our asses were hers if she heard that we had done anything improper in any way again. We went back to class, very nervous and proud of our *moms*. We held our heads high . . . and politely.

"Whooooooo Wheeeee, that was some meeting."

* * *

This has been a year of unimaginable experiences. The popular girl in my homeroom had to drop out of school because she got caught by the Big Bird—not revealing it until it was too late to have anything done about it. Now how dumb is that? I thought they had all the sense . . . It seems to me that we're more alike that they wish to think . . . . (That old saying "money talks, well having money and influence could get you anything, including abortion, which being black with no money and no influence, well, you get the picture.)

Our girl group bonded tighter than ever—we were inseparable. Olive and I went back to the snack shop owned by Mr. Gardner and to the bus terminal's black section, so as not to provoke anymore trouble. We never went back to the other one, even though some of the white kids begged us to come.

Chapter Forty-Seven

GRADUATION

After the meeting, Olive and I were very popular with the black boys and girls and had gained respect from some of the white kids who were afraid of showing their respect. The black kids all were asking us about the incident. We told them very frankly that we had broken down barriers for all of us, and that doing so gave us more confidence to stand up. But we also told them if they were not willing to stand for themselves, then we weren't going to do it for them.

Our girl posse was sitting in one of the booths at the bus terminal one day, when in walked Mr. Dumb-Dumb—that "Mark" fellow.

Needless to say, he spoke especially to me, saying he hadn't seen me at my aunt's for a while.

I said something like "So . . ."

He sat at the counter and offered to buy all of our lunches. Everyone accepted, except me.

"Girl, you crazy! You can save your quarter for something else," the gang whispered. I told them about the incident of the window washing. I had not forgotten to mention it; I had just thought it was insignificant.

They laughed as Pearlie said, "Oooh, ClaraBy, he's got a *thang* for you!"

"Well, he can keep his *thang* for me. He's an *old* man—every bit of twenty or so, and I don't want no ole man."

"Well . . ." Sylvia whispered, "I'll take him if you don't want him."

"Oh, girl, please." I smirked.

"You see the way he's dressed? He's probably a coal miner, and you know they make good money," Carolyn said.

"Yeah," Olive replied, "with a house full of kids and a fat wife, while he's out here mack-daddying. They all alike."

"Who cares?" I said smartly. "He's too old for one thing. So there, that's enough for me."

After that, it seemed as if he was there at least once every week. He was like a bad penny. But I finally accepted his offer to buy my lunch . . . big mistake!

* * *

Junior was graduating from high school. Thea-Thea and I went to the graduation, our first ever. The stage was full of dignified people as they called out each graduate's name.

Finally the principal called, "Calvin Mickens." Thea-Thea jumped up and screamed. "DAT'S MY BABY! DAT ONE'S MINE!" she cried. The crowd roared with laughter. She was beaming with pride.

The whole family was so proud of him, as he was the first of six to graduate. My brothers sent him money and told him he could come to Missouri with them if he wanted to.

When Oscar had come for him, Frank had gone back with him to Missouri. Thea-Thea was a happy woman with her boys together without those she-devils. But old habits die hard, and they had found two more.

Saturday morning after graduation, Daddy and Thea-Thea had gotten up earlier than usual. Thea-Thea fixed the usual big breakfast. Daddy went to the front porch and whistled his loud whistle, and out the door they came—those who could run and walk. By now, Paula was a big girl helping with the little ones. She had the baby on her hip as she made her way up the hill. Daddy said, "Here they come, HoneyBabe." And they hit the door throwing down anything that obstructed them from getting to the table.

Fried chicken smothered in gravy, fried potatoes and onions, fried apples in yum-yum syrup, and hot, hot biscuits. Now you talking about good, there is not a word in the dictionary to describe my Thea-Thea's cooking.

Daddy sat at the head of the table with Junior at the other end; Thea-Thea, me, and the kids all around. Daddy looked so proud as we held hands and he blessed the food.

Then, it was on. Paula started it off: "Hummmmmmmm-hummmmmmmm." Don't ask me why, but they all hummed when they ate. It was hilarious. They were deep in thought as they ate. Cute, cute, cute.

Daddy and Thea-Thea had Mr. Judd to pick them up by ten o'clock, as they were on their way downtown. They never said they had any business or anything, Thea-Thea just said, "Have da kitchen clean when we git back, ClaraBy. And don't y'all leave till we git back," she said as she went out the door. The kids had gotten their bellies full and took off giving kisses and hugs on their way.

"Yes, ma'am," I said, as if I had a choice.

Junior knew his chores, so we went about doing them, us asking each other why they had to go down the road.

Junior said, "I hope nothing is wrong—they seemed to be in a hurry."

Well, lo and behold, some time later, we heard a car pull up, and it was not Mr. Judd. It was a little black car at the foot of the hill with Mr. Man driving. Out stepped Thea-Thea and Daddy.

They had gone and bought a little secondhand car for Junior and me! Junior was beyond tickled. He was walking around the car with his hand over his mouth, smothering his "Hooooo, Hooooo!"

He said, "Baby Girl, I'm gonna teach ya real good how to drive. Now I know you think you already know how, but there's a difference when it comes to a *real* car. But . . . I'll show you, 'cause I'm going to be leaving soon, and you'll need to know how to drive Daddy and Thea-Thea around."

Mr. Man had taken him to get his license some time back, so he was well prepared for the evening out as he dashed off, hollering, "Don't worry, I'll be careful!"

Thea-Thea stood on the porch with a look of horror, knowing that he was going off by himself. Daddy just rocked back and forth, proud of what he saw.

Junior was ready for the world. He said, "I'm going into the armed services like Russell, and finish getting my education—maybe become a doctor or something," he said.

So here we were again at the bus station with my closest-in-age brother going off to boot camp. Now I knew all about who the man was in the picture, but I still prayed that he would treat Junior like his own kin.

The very same thing happened as when Russell left. Thea-Thea and Daddy had their cry, between hugs and kisses. Me too, and I'm all alone now. The Baby Girl.

Chapter Forty-Eight

HAD ENOUGH

Daddy was acting a little strange lately. I mean, he's missed work a couple of times in one month, and that is very unusual. Thea-Thea was trying to get him to go to the doctor, but he kept saying he'd be all right. He was sitting at the table holding his head one morning as I got up. He hadn't gone to work again. Now this is getting to be a bit too much.

"What's the matter, Daddy?" I asked.

"Oh, Baby Girl, I thank it's time I retired. I done told 'em at da mines. I's past old enough, and I just ain't feeling da best lately, and I thank my body telling me it's time."

"Oh, Daddy," I replied, "I agree—it's time."

"Yeah, HoneyBabe thanks we oughta go to da social security place and git it started. We need ya to take us, so ya can 'splain thangs."

"Yes, sir, Daddy, we'll go today, right away, right now." I ran upstairs to start getting dressed. I was ready for this, 'cause Daddy deserved to rest.

Off we went in the little used car Daddy had bought.

I had learned to drive almost from the day I could walk. Being curious as I was, whenever I got the chance, I would observe how the feet were used and the hands were maneuvered. I felt that I could even drive a big bus, as Junior who was always making a play bus with me the only passenger, getting on and off at every stop until I screamed, "Enough! You be the passenger and let me drive now!"

He was fascinated by the bus drivers. He would take any chair he could find and pretend that they were the seats on the bus.

I hadn't earned my license yet, but I knew it would be a cinch when the time came. So off we went to the Social Security office to sign Daddy up for his retirement. There were forms to be filled out and questions to be answered that Daddy and Thea-Thea had no idea how to do. He had a hard time climbing all of the steps up to the office. His breathing had gotten so bad.

"My baby is so smart," Daddy said. "We very blessed to have ya, ClaraBy," he said softly. When he called me by my name, it seemed as if he was highly respecting me as a young lady, not a baby anymore.

"Thank you, Daddy, and I'm very, very blessed to have you and Thea-Thea . . ." my voice cracking a little as I choked back the tears, trying not to imagine life without them . . . .

* * *

Water supply had gotten very low to none at all in our community. The well had long since dried up, and running water in the houses was almost down to a dribble. If anyone's water came on, the community would gather at that house with any container they had to fill. Women would bring their dirty clothes and wash them at the house where the water supply was.

The mines had slacked down; people were moving away, looking for work . . . My brother-in-law had found another job in the mines in Kentucky, and he, my sister, and their family had already moved to another county about fifty miles away. My brothers Frank and Oscar were together. Russell was making a career out of the army. Junior had graduated and joined the United States Army, too. Hot dog. Now there was just Daddy, Thea-Thea, and me.

My Ludie was gone. Mr. G-Baby was gone. Even Ms. Maxwell and Ms. Minnie had died. Who would have ever thought?

The Monroes had moved away. Janice and her family moved away last year. On and on and on.

God, what's happening? The world was spinning so fast. Everything was changing so rapidly . . . for the better, I prayed.

"Child, did you hear the latest?" Ms. Nellie spouted breathlessly as she came up the steps.

"What?" Thea-Thea asked eagerly.

"The law is catching 'em left and right. They finding out who married and who ain't and *jailing* 'em, honey. Common-law somethang or other. Well, heee, heeeeeeee, to beat it all, Reverend and his *wife*—we thought—just sneaked off and got married this morning!"

"WHAT?!" screamed Thea-Thea. "Ya mean he been deceiving us for all these years! Da dirty dog, "MAY DA GOOD LAWD HAVE MERCY ON 'EM! 'CAUSE HE CAN'T TELL ME *NUN-THIN* NO MO', AND I MEAN NO MO'! Talkin' 'bout low-down . . . now dat's low down. Here we is thanking he all upstanding an' all. Ya mean dem kids won't ligit? I wonder what he gon' tell his flock now. UHM, UHM, UHM, some people . . ." she mumbled.

Now it seemed that there were several couples that we thought was so hotty-totty, had been hanky-pankying all these years.

"Child, can't nobody say nothin' 'bout nobody, ya hear me."

They were deep in conversation when I heard Thea-Thea ask, "Nellie, what you and Slim gon' do?"

Ms. Nellie shook her head. "Child, we's been thanking 'bout da same thang. Slim trying like Cal to git his pension and stuff, but it's hard gittin up and down da road wit no car." She sighed and said, "I sho' don't wanna go to no big city, so I guess we's just got to tough it out till we can move outa this God-forsaken holla."

"Now, Nellie, you and Slim can use da car anytime ya need to, so don't keep making 'scuses, 'cause life toooo short, child, and ya gonna be left up here by yo'self."

"Girl," said Ms. Nellie, "have ya ever seen a place go down like this? I thought I'd never see da day dat it would be like this. Uhm, Uhm, Uhm."

Thea-Thea said, "I know what ya mean, honey-child; it seems so strange and quiet since my grandchilluns left, but Lawd, its sho' been peaceful . . . !" They laughed loudly.

"I know one thang," said Ms. Nellie. "When Slim git home this evening, we gonna have a serious talk, 'cause, I ain't gonna stay up in dis hollow wit prac'cally ever'body gone."

Chapter Forty-Nine

Yippee!

Thea-Thea came home from down the road one sunny afternoon, and Daddy said, "How'd it go, HoneyBabe?"

"Good," she said, "very good. We got it!"

"What the world? What the world?! Got what?" I screamed.

"Da house, child, da house! We gon' move outa this holla as soon as we can git packed.... We're moving down da road just across da highway from your aunt Cellie!" She was ecstatic.

Daddy said softly, "Thank da Lawd, thank da Lawd..."

Yes, it would be a very interesting time coming. Well, this was the life in my little coal-camp hollow. I'd seen a lot of changes, but my life was just beginning, and I had a feeling that it was going to be a *pret-ty*, interesting one...

My daddy retired and drawing his checks—I got a check, Thea-Thea got a check, and *we were moving on up*, heeee, heeeeeeee!

Life was really *loooking goooood*...!

Thank you, Jesus!

... To be continued ...

Ohhhhh *yeah!*
HELLO WORLD! HERE COME CLARABY ROSE!